The dog hurtled toward me. He wasn't even a little bit scary. He just looked really, really excited to say hello.

Which is what he did, by leaping up and planting his paws on my shoulders and licking my face all over.

"Ew, GROSS!" Katie yelled.

"It's OK," I said. I got on my knees and the dog sat down in front of me. His tail went *thump thump thump* on the porch. This dog had the hugest grin I'd ever seen. I got the weird feeling he agreed with me about how dopey Katie and Sarah were.

"Come in and I'll get you his stuff," Katie said. "We got a crate for him, but good luck keeping him inside it!"

Get into some
Pet Trouble

Pet Trouble

Runaway Retriever

by T.T. SUTHERLAND

SCHOLASTIC INC.

New York   Toronto   London   Auckland   Sydney
Mexico City   New Delhi   Hong Kong   Buenos Aires

No part of this publication may be reproduced, stored in a retrieval system, or transmitted in any form or by any means, electronic, mechanical, photocopying, recording, or otherwise, without written permission of the publisher. For information regarding permission, write to Scholastic Inc., Attention: Permissions Department, 557 Broadway, New York, NY 10012.

ISBN-13: 978-0-545-10241-4
ISBN-10: 0-545-10241-3

12 11 10 9 8 7 6 5 4 3 2 1   9 10 11 12 13 14/0

Printed in the U.S.A.
First printing, April 2009

For George and Virginia — TTS

CHAPTER 1

It was pasta primavera night, about a week before school started, when I first heard about the dog.

I remember because I was stuck in the kitchen for, like, five hours while my older sister, Camellia, insisted on teaching me how to make pasta primavera. I tried to tell her it was pointless. Dad and I were never going to chop vegetables. Once she was gone, we were going to eat frozen pizza every night. Or frozen lasagna. Or Chinese takeout. *Maybe* we would micro-wave some frozen green beans and eat them with our spaghetti and meatballs. Dad and I both thought this was a pretty good plan. In fact, the only good thing I could see about Camellia going off to college was that Dad and I would get to eat meat again.

My sister decided at the beginning of the summer that we should all be vegetarians. She said all her future roommates at Oberlin would be "absolutely horrified" if they found out she ate meat. Dad and I didn't try to argue with her. We figured it was only for a couple of months anyway. Maybe less, Dad said, if we were lucky and it was "just a phase" (it wasn't). So I went over to Eric's or Troy's whenever I really wanted hamburgers (which it turns out is like four times a week, but they don't mind).

Camellia wasn't too excited to hear about our frozen pizza plan, though, not even when I promised we'd get pizza with healthy stuff on it. She started whacking at the zucchini extra hard. I moved to the other side of the kitchen island with the carrots. I've been hit by flying zucchini before when Camellia gets worked up about something.

I know she's just worried about us. Mom divorced Dad and left when I was five and Camellia was twelve, so she's kind of taken care of me and Dad since then. She thinks we're going to totally fall apart without her. I think it's going to be a lot quieter around here. But I bet we can handle it.

Out of the blue, Camellia said: "Parker, you're a dog person, right?"

"A dog person?" I said. "Isn't that, like, an oxymoron?" I was pretty proud of using that word. We'd learned it in Ms. Applebaum's fifth-grade class last year. It means a phrase where the two words sound like opposites, like "serious fun" or "jumbo shrimp" or "delicious zucchini."

Camellia didn't notice my keen literary skills. "I mean, do you like dogs?"

I shrugged. "Sure. Everyone likes dogs."

"Well, some people are cat people," Camellia said, scooping the zucchini slices into a colander. "So they like cats better."

"OK. I like cats, too," I said.

"Which do you like better?"

This seemed like a weird question to me. We'd never had any pets, so it was like asking me if I liked basketball or football better. I play baseball. I don't have an opinion about other sports.

"The same, I guess," I said.

Camellia made one of her irritated noises. "Par*ker.* Fine. Well, *I* think you're a dog person."

"OK," I said. I went to check on the pot of water, which still wasn't boiling.

"I mean, because you like to run around outside and you have lots of friends. I think if you were a cat person you'd be more private and quiet."

That was kind of funny. I think I'm a pretty quiet guy, actually. My theory is, if you don't say too much, you're less likely to make people mad. Mostly I just agree with what people say. I think that's why I have all those friends she's talking about.

Also, guys don't care if you're quiet. It's only girls

who are like, "What? What are you thinking? What does that face mean?" when you're not even doing anything.

This conversation was a good example of how I always agree with people, actually, because the next thing I said was, "Yeah, I guess you're right. I am a dog person."

Camellia beamed. "That's what I told Dad," she said. "That's why I'm getting you a dog."

Now she had my attention. "What?" I said. "Why? What?"

She wiped her hands dry on her pink-and-green-striped apron. "You guys are going to be lonely without me," she said. "Especially you. So I decided you need a dog to keep you company while I'm gone."

"Dad won't be lonely," I said. "He has Julianne."

Camellia made a face and then tried to hide it. But I knew she didn't like Dad's new girlfriend either. He hadn't dated anyone since Mom left, so it was really weird to suddenly have a strange person hanging out with us. Julianne has dark red hair that Camellia says is definitely dyed. We both got Dad's cocoa-brown hair instead of Mom's superblond, and Camellia says she would never change it, not even if everyone else at Oberlin dyes their hair bright green. Julianne is an artist or something. Dad met her a month ago when she went into his bank to apply for a loan for her art studio. I heard Camellia call her a "ditz" on the phone once, even though she tried to be nice when Julianne was around. Which was way too often, if you asked me.

"Julianne might not stick around," Camellia said. "I mean, a month isn't long enough to tell if it'll last. And dogs are better than girlfriends anyway. You might as well learn that now." Camellia's boyfriend had broken up with her a few weeks earlier because he was going to the University of Miami, so she was in kind of a major anti-relationship mood.

"What did Dad say about this plan?" I asked.

"He said I should talk to you about it," Camellia said, pulling out her cell phone and hitting one of the speed-dial buttons. "But of course I was right. I *knew* you'd be excited."

I guess my "excited" face probably looks a lot like my "confused" face. "How would we take care of a —" I started to say, but she held up one finger and turned away from me.

"Katie?" she said into the phone. Katie is Camellia's best friend. She's going to Mount Holyoke and they spent the whole summer talking about how "absolutely devastating" it is that they'll be so far apart and "You better text me all the time" and "I'll still be your

#1 Facebook friend, right?" and all that. Personally, I'd be surprised if Katie even remembers to take her cell phone to college with her. She's totally scatter-brained — pretty much the complete opposite of Camellia.

"Guess what?" Camellia went on. "They said yes! Yeah! Totally!"

Uh-oh.

"I know, it *is* the best idea. When can we come get him?"

I waved my hands frantically, but Camellia didn't seem to notice. Or if she did, she pretended not to.

She frowned. "Oh, no! How long ago?" Pause. "Wow, aren't you worried? Shouldn't you go out look-ing for him?" She glanced at me. I tried to make a *hey, shouldn't we talk about this* face, but that didn't get through to her either. "Really? Are you sure? OK. Well, call me when you find him. We can come get him tomorrow, maybe. Great! OK, you too! Byeee!"

Camellia snapped the phone shut and tucked it in her jeans pocket again. "This is so perfect," she said. "Parker, you're totally going to love this dog!"

"What dog?" I said. "Katie doesn't have a dog."

"Yes, she does," Camellia said. "She got it a month ago. Well, it was supposed to be for her and Sarah together, but Sarah doesn't want it, and now Katie's going off to college, so they're looking for a new home for him. And so I was like, I know, he'd be perfect for Parker! He's so gorgeous, Parker, seriously."

First of all, I never knew dogs could be "gorgeous." Frankly, that sounded a little ominous to me. It would be just like Camellia to give me something small and fluffy and silly-looking that my friends will laugh and laugh at. Secondly, if Katie's fifteen-year-old sister didn't want it, why would I?

OK. I'll admit I was a little curious. One of the guys on my baseball team, Hugo, has this totally funny mutt whose name is Scratcher, but Hugo always calls him Squashface. He seems like a pretty cool dog. And I once saw a thing on TV where these dogs were chasing Frisbees in some kind of competition, and that looked kind of cool, too. Maybe this dog would do that with me.

"So why can't we go see him now?" I asked.

Camellia took the pasta and poured it into the pot, but she did it in this kind of shifty way that made me think she was trying not to tell me something. "Oh, it's nothing," she said. "He just runs away some-times. But Katie says he always shows up again by the next day."

I couldn't believe it. "They just let their dog run around the neighborhood?" I said. "They don't go looking for him?"

"Katie says they used to, at first, but since he does it all the time, they just gave up." She stirred the pasta busily. Aha. I was starting to figure this out. No wonder Katie's family didn't want him. They didn't like anything that made them get up off the couch.

"Anyway," Camellia went on, "it's no big deal. Our yard has a better fence than theirs, so I'm sure he won't do that here."

"What's his name?" I asked.

Camellia shrugged. "I don't know," she said. "I think they call him Dog."

That made up my mind. This poor dog obviously needed to be rescued. If Katie and Sarah were my owners, I'd run away, too.

"All right," I said. "Tomorrow we'll go get him."

I was getting a dog . . . whether I liked it or not.

CHAPTER 2

As soon as we rang the doorbell, I heard barking.

"Shut up!" someone yelled, probably Katie. "Shut up! Dog! Shut up! SARAH! PUT HIM OUTSIDE! SAAAARAAAH!"

"I'M DOING IT!" Sarah yelled back.

Dad looked really nervous. He kept saying, "Are you sure about this?" When he heard all the noise, his face went kind of white. But I wasn't worried. I've been to Katie's house a couple of times, and it's always like that, since way before they had a dog. Sometimes I think Camellia likes it over there because all the yelling makes it so different from our house.

The barking got farther away, and then finally the front door opened and Katie was standing there.

"Camellia!" she shrieked happily, the way she does every single time they see each other. "And Parker, oh my gosh, when did you get so tall?" She saw me about two weeks ago, but normally she doesn't talk to me much. And maybe I'd grown since then. She reached past me to shake Dad's hand. "Hi Mr. Green, great to see you. Come in, you guys!"

But as Camellia stepped forward, suddenly I heard the barking again — only it was coming from behind us now. I turned around just as a dog came galloping around the side of the house at full speed.

He was not small or fluffy or silly-looking. He was a big, brown-eyed golden retriever with long, shining, sun-colored fur, and he was running straight at me.

"OH MY GOSH, SARAAAH!" Katie hollered. "You left the gate open again!"

"I DID NOT!" Sarah screamed from the back of the house.

"Well, now we're never going to catch him!" Katie yelled.

Something made me open my arms as the dog hurtled toward me. I mean, he wasn't even a little bit scary. He just looked really, really excited to say hello.

Which is what he did, by leaping up and planting his paws on my shoulders and licking my face all over.

"Ew, GROSS!" Katie yelled. She reached to grab his collar. "Get DOWN, Dog, OFF! Leave Parker alone!"

"It's OK," I said. I got on my knees and the dog sat down in front of me. His tail went *thump thump thump* on the porch. I didn't even know dogs could smile, but this dog had the hugest grin I'd ever seen. He looked like someone had poured sunshine all over him.

"You're such a pain in my butt, Dog," Katie said, putting her hands on her hips.

"Woof!" the dog said, tossing back his head so his long silky ears flapped. He grinned at me. I got the weird feeling he agreed with me about how dopey Katie and Sarah were.

"Come in and I'll get you his stuff," Katie said. Dad started to say something, but she kept on talking right over him. "We got a crate for him, but good luck keeping him inside it!"

Camellia and Dad followed Katie inside. When I stood up to go in, the dog came with me. He poked his nose into my hand and made a *whuffl*ing noise. His head was smooth and soft when I petted it. He stayed beside me as we followed Katie around the house. She had already filled a plastic bag with dog food and a leash and two half-chewed rawhide bones. In the kitchen she picked up his metal water bowl, emptied it into the sink, and put that in the bag, too.

Sarah came stomping in from the backyard. "I totally did not leave the gate open, Katie."

"That's what you said last time!" Katie said.

"Yeah! Because it was true last time, too!"

"So what, he just teleports through the fence?"

"Whatever!" Sarah snapped. "I just know it's not *my* fault!"

"Girls, girls," their mom said, coming into the kitchen. She said hi to us and immediately started thanking Dad for taking the dog off their hands. Dad looked kind of uncomfortable, but he's about as bad at saying no as I am. The dog poked my leg with his nose, looked pointedly at the back door, and then looked up at me.

"Can I take him outside?" I asked.

"Sure," Katie said. "Just make sure the gate is closed."

Sarah stuck out her tongue at her sister. I held the door open for the dog. He immediately bounded down the steps and raced across the yard. I was hoping I'd see him get through the fence so I could figure out how he did it. But he kept circling back around to me instead of trying to escape.

Their fence was made of wood and was only as high as my waist. Maybe he could jump right over it.

Our fence was chain-link metal and nearly as tall as me. No way would he get over that.

I walked around the yard, looking at the fence. The dog trotted beside me, wagging his tail the whole time. The sun lit up his fur like fire.

The gate near the front of the house was closed. But as I came closer, I saw something. There was an outdoor storage chest set up against the fence. It looked like the one Troy's dad used to keep his garden tools in.

As I walked up to it, the dog ran over and jumped up on top of it. He shook out his fur and sat down. He looked very proud of himself. I could see that from there it would be supereasy to jump over the fence, even if you were a lot smaller than a golden retriever.

"You're pretty clever, aren't you?" I said, sitting on the chest beside him. He lay down on his side and put his head on my knee, panting happily. I scratched behind his ears. "You're much cleverer than Katie and Sarah, that's for sure," I said. "I can't believe they didn't see this. I guess they don't think like us, huh?"

The dog looked up at me with his big brown eyes.

"Well," I said, "if you're coming home with me, you're going to need a real name."

His tail swished back and forth like he understood me.

"I've been reading this book about King Arthur," I said to him. "I bet you'd make a great knight of the Round Table." He did have a really noble-looking face. And then I had the best idea. He was more than a knight — he was a wizard, magically escaping whenever Katie put him outside. Of course, I'd figured out how the magic worked, but it was still a mystery to everyone else.

"Merlin," I said. His tail thumped. I think he liked it. "All right, clever dog. I'm going to call you Merlin."

CHAPTER 3

Dad was worried about what we were going to do once school started again on Monday. He had to go to work all day — he manages a bank in the next town over — and I'd be gone from seven a.m. to three p.m. I suggested maybe I could come home at lunchtime to let Merlin out, because my school was only a few blocks away. But Dad said he didn't think the school would like that.

"You guys are such worrywarts," Camellia said.

I thought that was unfair. Dad was the one worrying, not me. I was the one coming up with excellent ideas. How cool would it be to come home in the middle of the day to see my dog? (*My* dog. That sounded so strange.) Any excuse to leave school would be awesome, if you asked me.

But Camellia, of course, had the most logical solution. "You can just leave him in the yard while you're out," she said. "We'll put water out there and he can run around all he wants. That way there won't be any accidents in the house. Lots of people have outdoor dogs that never come inside."

"He'll be inside with us when we're home, though," I said. We were driving home from Katie's, and Merlin was sitting in the backseat with me. He had his nose stuck up near the top of the window, which was cracked open. I wanted to roll it down and let him stick his head out. I've seen lots of dogs hang their heads out the car window so the wind could blow in their faces.

But along with the dog food and the dog bed, Katie had given us a stack of dog books about a mile high. I thought this was another sign of her being crazy. If you spent all your time reading those books, when would you hang out with your dog? But Camellia loves books. If there were a book for each decision she had to make, she would read them all before doing anything.

So of course it started the minute we got in the car. As I went to roll down the window, she said, "No, don't do that." She held up a chapter on car trips. "See, it isn't safe for the dog. Something could blow into its eyes."

"Poor Merlin," I said, rumpling his golden fur. "No fun for you."

"He should really be in his crate," she fussed, flipping pages.

"It's only a ten-minute drive," Dad said. "I think we'll be all right. Hey, maybe we should have Julianne over later to meet him. She loves dogs."

"Sure, whatever," Camellia said, which is her way of saying no without getting in trouble. "Here, this is important." Camellia twisted around to read to me. "This says not to let the dog sleep on your bed at first. It has to know that you're the alpha dog — you know, like, the boss."

"I'm the boss," I said to Merlin. He turned his head around and smiled at me. *Thump thump* went his tail on the gray car seat.

"The boss gets the best bed," Camellia said, "and the other members of the pack have to sleep on the floor."

"I think that means Camellia should sleep on the floor tonight, too, don't you?" I said to Merlin. "Just so it's clear who the boss in the house is."

"Ha ha," Camellia said. "Maybe we should put him in his crate. Otherwise he might jump up on your bed while you're sleeping."

"That seems so sad," I said, picturing Merlin alone in his crate in the dark. "And cramped." The cage was supposed to be the right size for golden retrievers, but it looked awfully small to me. I wouldn't want to be stuck in there all night.

"I bet we still have a baby gate in the garage somewhere," Dad said. "If we can find that, we could just block off the kitchen and leave him in there."

I didn't see a problem with him sleeping in my room, but Camellia can be really persistent when she thinks she knows the answer to something. So when we got home, Dad and I went into the garage and dug through piles and piles of old boxes. It's crazy how much stuff is in there. We can't even fit the car in the garage anymore. It's just storage for stuff none of us have used for a hundred years.

Merlin loved it. He stuck his nose into every box. He knocked over the rake by accident and then barked and barked at it. He found a bag of toys from when we were kids and managed to chew off one of the arms of Camellia's old teddy bear before we caught him and took it away. We decided not to tell Camellia about that.

Dad was right, though. Finally we found the baby gate leaning against the wall behind a bunch of file boxes. It was white with little blue handles at the top. When I saw it, I had this weird flash of memory of Mom putting it up so I'd stay in the kitchen while she vacuumed the living room. I had freaked out . . . it was like being in a cage, with loud roaring outside. I hoped Merlin would handle it better than I had. Poor guy.

The gate was kind of dusty, so we took it out into the yard to hose it down. Merlin went totally wild with happiness when the water started spraying out of the hose. He barked and jumped at the spray like he was trying to pin it down. He chased it around in circles as Dad tried to turn it away from him. He ran through it over and over again like a little kid in a fountain. And of course, as soon as he was soaking wet, he came galloping over and shook himself right next to us.

Dad rolled his eyes and went inside to change and dry off the gate. I decided to stay in the yard with Merlin for a while longer. He seemed so excited to be out there. Once Dad was gone, I sprayed Merlin a few more times with the hose, since he liked it so much.

"Whoa," said a voice by the fence. "Hey, Parker, what's going on?" It was my friend Danny Sanchez, who lives a couple of blocks away. He's got spiky black hair and he's taller than I am and he's, like, Mr. Active. He's on all the sports teams at school. I think he rides around the neighborhood five times a day all summer just to burn off all the energy he's got.

Danny climbed off his bike and leaned on the fence, staring at Merlin in surprise.

"We got a dog," I said.

"Yeah, I see that!" he said, laughing.

I opened the gate and let him in. Merlin immediately came over and sniffed Danny up and down. "What's his name?" Danny asked.

"Merlin," I said. I told him the story of how we got him.

"I can't *wait* for us to get a dog," Danny said. "Mom says maybe this year, if we all promise to help take care of it, but the problem is we all want different things." That's usually the problem in Danny's house. Danny has three older brothers — Carlos, Miguel, and Oliver — and a younger sister, Rosie. There is no good way to get them all to agree on anything. Especially Rosie. She's ten, a year below us, but she is bossier than most of the girls in our grade. She's even bossier than Camellia sometimes.

Merlin wagged his tail as Danny and I stood there patting him. He kept looking back and forth between us like he wanted to be part of our conversation. He was still pretty wet, his long fur dripping water into the grass. I liked that Danny didn't mind patting a wet dog. He's cool like that.

"I want a dog like this," Danny said. "Or a Lab, maybe. Something that will run around and chase a ball with me."

"I'm taking him to the park tomorrow," I said. "Want to come?"

"Sure!" Danny said.

Dad called me to come inside, so Merlin and I said 'bye to Danny. As soon as Camellia saw us, she cried, "Don't move! Stay right there! Not another step!" We stood there dripping while she ran around getting towels. I held on to Merlin's collar, because I could tell he was excited to go sniffing around his new house.

As soon as we toweled him off and let him go, he started running from room to room, poking his nose into everything and wagging his tail. I left my shoes by the door and went to wash my hands. By the time I got to my room, Merlin was on my bed, rolling damply around on my dark green bedspread and looking very pleased with himself.

"Oh, thanks a lot," I said, laughing.

"See?" Camellia said, coming up behind me. "He's trying to assert his dominance. You shouldn't let him do that. Merlin, off!"

Merlin promptly flopped over on his side with his head on the pillow. He gave us a mischievous sideways grin. He took up nearly the whole bed, especially with his tail swishing back and forth.

"It's OK, I got it," I said. Camellia went "hrrmph" and stomped back to the kitchen. "Come on, boy," I said, "let's go unpack your stuff." He jumped off the bed right away and followed me into the living room, where we had left the dog things in a pile.

The weirdest thing about all the stuff Katie had given us was that there were lots of books and food, but no toys that I could see. I hunted through the plastic bags, which was funny because every time I picked up a new one, Merlin would come scrambling over to stick his nose inside. But there wasn't anything for us to play with. He got pretty excited about the rawhide bones, though, so I let him wrestle one out of the bag. He flopped down and started chewing on it with a big goofy grin.

"Don't worry, Merlin," I said, scratching his head, "tomorrow we'll find a tennis ball or Frisbee for you."

His crate was this big metal contraption that folded flat. As soon as I started to unfold it, Merlin dropped the bone and went tearing out of the room like someone had just lit his tail on fire. I guessed I would feel the same way if someone started unfolding a classroom in the middle of my house.

I finished setting it up and then shoved it into a corner of the living room, out of the way. Maybe if Merlin saw that he didn't *have* to go into it, he would be less worried about it. Then I went looking for him and found him lying on my bed again. He put his head on his paws and looked up at me with huge woeful eyes. It was like he was saying *Please, please don't put me in my crate.*

"Don't worry," I said, sitting down next to him. "We'll only put you in there if we have to."

"Dinner!" Camellia called from downstairs. "We're having tofu burgers! You guys will love them!"

I rubbed Merlin's head. "See, things could be worse. At least there's meat in *your* dinner."

Dad hadn't mentioned inviting Julianne over again, so we had a stranger-free evening. Camellia spent all of dinner reading to us from the dog books while Dad and I covered our tofu burgers in ketchup and pretended they were great.

"Most dogs love their crates," Camellia said. "It's like another den to them."

"Not Merlin," I said.

"Where did Katie's family get him from?" my dad asked.

"They saw an ad in the *Gazette*," Camellia said. "The couple who owned him decided to move to an apartment in the city that wouldn't allow dogs."

"So they picked an apartment over their dog?" I said. "Poor Merlin." He was lying under my chair.

I leaned down to scratch his head. "You're lucky to be away from people like that."

"You shouldn't talk to him at the dinner table," Camellia lectured. "Or he might start to beg."

But Merlin was a much better dog than that. He licked my hand, but he didn't try to bother any of us for food. He waited patiently until dinner was over and we put down his own food, and then he ate the whole bowlful.

We set up his bed in the kitchen. It was pretty much just a giant blue beanbag with little white paw prints all over it. He sniffed it and nosed it and walked around it a few times, then looked up at me like, *Really? But your bed seems much more comfortable.*

"Sorry, buddy," I said, crouching to give him a hug. "I'm sure you'll sleep fine in here, though."

"Of course he will," Camellia said. "Come on, let's make it seem normal."

I followed her out into the hall, and Dad set the baby gate across the open doorway. Merlin came to the other side and looked up at me, wagging his tail. He poked the baby gate with his nose, but it stayed put. It was as high as Katie's fence, but here there wasn't anything he could jump up onto get over it.

"Good night, Merlin," I said, turning off the hall light. "See you tomorrow."

CHAPTER 4

That night I had the dream I sometimes have about my mom, which is weird, because I don't even really remember her, and we haven't heard from her in six years. In the dream, I'm sitting in a parked car watching her walk away. She's wearing a green raincoat. So I guess it's raining. And I'm alone in the car with a bag of groceries that's all different kinds of cookies, chocolate-chip and Oreos and peanut butter and stuff. I don't know, it's a pretty stupid dream.

Then I felt something breathing on me, and I woke up.

When I opened my eyes, I saw Merlin's nose about an inch away from my own. It was morning. His golden head was on my pillow. He was lying on top of the covers, snuggled up close to me. When he saw me open my eyes, I felt his tail start thumping madly against the mattress.

"Uh-oh," I said. "You're going to be in big trouble, mister."

He scooted his head a little bit closer and licked my nose.

"Eeurgh," I said, laughing and rubbing my face. "Not with me, silly. Camellia's the one you have to suck up to."

He rolled and wriggled sideways until all his paws were up in the air. He was pressed up next to me with his ears flopped over backward. I put my arm around him and rubbed his belly.

"Poor Merlin," I said. "People keep leaving you, huh? Don't worry. I won't do that."

"WHAT IS THIS?" Camellia demanded from the doorway.

Merlin lifted his head and gave her a startled, big-eyed, *what'd I do?* expression. She crossed her arms. He started flailing madly until he got himself right side up again. Then he bounded off the bed and over to Camellia, wagging his tail and bouncing around her. Even she couldn't resist that grin. Grudgingly she patted him on the head.

"PARKER," Camellia said, apparently deciding it was easier to be mad at me. "I can't believe you let him sleep in here! You heard what the books said!"

"I didn't let him out!" I protested. "He was here when I woke up!"

"Yeah, right!" she said. "So how did he get out?"

I scrambled out of bed. "I don't know how he did it, but I swear I didn't know he was here until just now."

Dad came hurrying up the stairs. "The dog's gone!" he called as he got to the top. "He's not in the — oh." He spotted Merlin sitting happily beside Camellia. Dad scratched his head, looking confused. "Why'd you put the baby gate back up after letting him out?" he asked.

"I didn't," Camellia said. "He got out by himself, according to Parker. The gate's still up?"

We all went downstairs to look. I'd figured Merlin must have pushed the gate over somehow. But there it was, exactly as we'd left it. Merlin poked it with his nose again and then looked up at me, wagging his tail like, *I took care of this little problem, didn't I?*

"How'd he do that?" Dad said, rubbing his eyes.

"Maybe he just jumped over it," I said.

"We'll have to try something different tonight," Camellia said.

"All right," I said, although I still thought it was unnecessary. I really didn't feel like Merlin and I were locked in some kind of primal struggle for dominance.

After breakfast, I called Danny and Troy, and IM'ed Eric, who is always online. We only had a few days of summer left. I wanted to spend every minute that I could outside with Merlin.

Camellia didn't think it would be safe for me to ride my bike and have Merlin on a leash at the same time because he could "pull me over" or "get tangled in the wheels" or something like that. But I didn't mind. The park was close enough to walk. And oh boy, Merlin was *so* excited to see his leash, which was also blue with little white paw prints on it. He jumped and barked and ran around in circles and it took me about half an hour just to pin him down and clip it onto his collar.

Then on the way to the park he wanted to stop and smell every single bush and blade of grass, but that was OK with me. I like our neighborhood. It's really quiet and I know practically everyone. Old Mrs. Sibelius was sitting out on her front porch, and she waved at me like she always does. I took the long way around to go by Kristal Perkins's house. She's one of the few girls in our grade who isn't totally weird, and I thought she'd like to meet Merlin. She wasn't outside, but her little sister, Skye, was, reading on the porch steps.

"Oooooooooooh!" Skye yelped as soon as she saw Merlin. She put down her book and ran over to us. "Oh wow! Oh wow! Oh wow!" She stopped a foot away from Merlin and stared at him, kind of hopping up and down with excitement. Her blond ponytail bounced and bounced.

"Hey, Skye," I said. Skye is pretty cool, too, for a nine-year-old. "This is Merlin." I crouched beside him. "You can say hi. Here, let him smell you."

"You got a *dog*," Skye said wistfully, holding out her hand. Merlin snuffled her hand and then licked it. She laughed. "I wish we could have a dog."

"You can come play with him sometimes if you want," I said. "Is Kristal home?"

"No, she's at art camp all day," Skye said. "She's learning how to make movies. It's so unfair."

"Maybe you can do that next summer," I said. "Tell her I said hi, OK?"

"I will," Skye said, patting Merlin lightly on the head.

Next I stopped at Eric's house, which is pretty close to the park. His sisters were in the driveway playing basketball, but they didn't come over to say hi. They're sixteen and they always act like Eric and his friends have rabies. His mom came out to say hi and meet Merlin, though. She's the vet at the Paws and Claws Animal Hospital in town.

"He's beautiful," she said, stroking Merlin's long silky fur. "Let me know if you want to bring him in for a checkup anytime. I might be able to get you a discount." She winked at me.

"Thanks, Dr. Lee," I said.

"Mom, why can't I have a dog like this?" Eric asked.

"We have Odysseus and Ariadne," his mother said, pointing to the two long-haired cats that were watching us from the porch. Their eyes were narrow slits and their tails were lashing back and forth. They did *not* look pleased to see Merlin. But then, they never looked pleased to see anyone. They were kind of like Eric's sisters that way.

"*Those* are *cats*," Eric pointed out, "and *they* belong to Mercy and Faith. Plus, they hate me."

"They don't —" Dr. Lee started to say, but she stopped mid-sentence and shrugged. "Well, OK, but at least you know it's not personal."

Eric rolled his eyes. "We'll be at the park, Mom."

"All right," his mom said. "If you boys want to come back here for lunch, we can make grilled cheese. I might even have some ham to throw in, if you're lucky, Parker," she added with a smile. She knew all about the vegetarian regime going on at my house.

Danny and Troy were waiting for us at the baseball diamond in the park. Troy was so excited to meet Merlin, he accidentally knocked his own glasses off. We took Merlin into the dog run and let him off the leash. I'd walked past the dog run a million times, but I'd never been inside. It was actually a pretty big area of the park, all fenced off so the dogs could run without getting loose. There weren't any other dogs in there yet.

Danny ran up and down shouting, and Merlin ran after him, barking madly. Troy had remembered to bring a tennis ball, so we tried throwing that for Merlin. He loved it. He was awesome at chasing the ball down. Sometimes he even caught it in midair, like a pro outfielder! But he was not so great about bringing it back. We had to chase him down and wrestle it away from him most of the time. He thought this was pretty much the best game ever.

One of the cool things I didn't know about the dog run was that there's a water fountain in the middle of it. But not a regular water fountain. The water comes straight up from a hole in the ground when you step on a lever. There's a metal basin set into the stone that you can fill up. You can also lift the basin out to empty it if you want to.

The best thing about the fountain was that Merlin figured out pretty quick how to set off the water himself. He'd run over, step on the lever, and then dive forward to try and get into the spray before it disappeared again. Luckily he didn't succeed very often, although he did manage to flounder into the basin a couple of times.

Finally I put the leash back on him and we went to sit in our favorite spot, on a hill beside the baseball diamond. Merlin flopped down on the grass beside me and put his head on my knee. His chin fur was wet from splashing around in the basin, but I didn't mind. My jeans would survive.

"He's pretty smart," Troy said admiringly, pushing his glasses up his nose. People sometimes say Troy and I look like brothers, but I think that's only because they always see us together. His hair is kind of reddish, while mine is brown, and his eyes are blue, but mine are green. Plus I'm nearly six inches taller than he is. He keeps saying his "growth spurt" is sure to start in junior high. We've been friends since we were born, because our birthdays are only a couple days apart, and our moms were put in the same room at the hospital.

Except, of course, his mom is still around, and mine isn't. But that's OK. His mom is nice but kind of overprotective. Seriously, she texts him, like, once an hour to find out where he is.

"Merlin is supersmart," I agreed. "He's got supernatural powers or something." I told them about him escaping from Katie's yard. Then I told them about the baby gate and how he ended up on my bed anyway.

Troy got really excited. "We should figure out how he does it," he said. "It's like a mystery! We should solve it!" Troy *loves* detective stories. He's read all the Hardy Boys books and he's started reading some grown-up ones, too, but his mom has to approve them all first. He wants to solve crimes when he's older, like the guys on cop shows. (He's not allowed to watch most of those either, but he sees them sometimes at Danny's house. The rules there are a little less strict than everywhere else because there are so many people to keep track of.)

"It doesn't matter," I said. "Camellia's probably spent the whole day coming up with some new way to imprison him. Tonight he'll be sleeping alone. Sorry, buddy." I ruffled Merlin's fur and he made a funny snorting sound like, *We'll see about that!*

Sure enough, after dinner Camellia announced that she thought we should put Merlin in the bathroom overnight. She said we'd put his bed and some water in there and then close the door, and it would be totally fine.

I argued with her a bit, but finally I gave in. Because I knew something she didn't.

I knew that the night before . . . I had left my bedroom door closed.

CHAPTER 5

The next morning, there he was, snoring away on the pillow beside me. I grinned and scratched his head. He opened his eyes and licked my nose again.

"You're a very bad dog," I said to him. His tail thumped on the bed.

"WHAT?" I heard Camellia shriek from down the hall. She came tearing into my room. "How did he do that?" she demanded, pointing at Merlin. He sat up alertly. "How did he get out? Parker, did you — "

"I didn't!" I said. "I swear!"

Luckily Camellia believes me more than Katie believes Sarah. We have a rule about honesty in our house. She threw up her hands. "That is just crazy. You are crazy, dog."

Thump thump, went Merlin's tail.

"I'm leaving for college in two days," Camellia said. "If you haven't figured this out by then, I won't be here to help you."

I had forgotten that she was leaving so soon. I didn't like to think about it.

"Let's try it again and see if we can figure out what he's doing," I said.

Dad was already at work, so it was just the two of us. I got dressed and then we took Merlin down the hall and into the bathroom. He sat down on his bed on top of the bath mat and tilted his head at us like, *I don't get this game.* Camellia and I backed out of the bathroom and shut the door. We pretended like we were walking away, stomping our feet on the floorboards. Then we sat down a little ways away from the bathroom and watched the door.

First we heard the *jingle jingle* of the tags on Merlin's collar. Then we heard him snuffling along the bottom of the door. His claws went *scrabble scrabble* on the tiles like he was thinking about digging his way out. He made this sad little whining sound that made me want to jump up and let him out, but Camellia put one hand on my arm and motioned for me to wait.

Then we heard a thud. I guessed that Merlin had got up on his back paws with his front paws on the door. There were scratching noises and a few more little whimpers. He walked away from the door and then back again. Another thud. *Scrabble scrabble*

scrabble . . . and suddenly the knob turned and the door opened.

Merlin came bounding out. When he saw us he looked surprised and a little bit guilty, but then he galloped over and started licking our faces. His tail was swishing back and forth, and he barked happily a couple of times. I could tell he thought he'd won whatever game we were playing. He was *so* pleased with himself, it was impossible not to laugh at him.

"I've never seen anything like that," Camellia said, fending him off and standing up. "I think we're going to have to put him in his crate if we want him to stay put."

"He really hates his crate, though," I said. "Watch, I'll show you." I led Merlin downstairs into the living room. As soon as I walked toward his crate he crouched down low to the ground and then slowly started to sneak away. I'd noticed he always went in a big circle around the furniture to stay away from it.

"He *should* like it," Camellia said, catching his collar. He leaned against her, wagging his tail. "I wonder why he doesn't." She picked up one of the dog books from the coffee table and flipped through it. After a minute, she took out her phone and went into the kitchen. I could hear her calling Katie.

"It's all right, Merlin," I said, sitting down on the carpet next to him. "It's not so bad in there. Here, look." I crawled over to his crate and put my head inside. "See? It doesn't scare me."

Merlin stopped panting and cocked his head. He looked kind of confused.

"Nothing to worry about," I said. "You're being a big 'fraidy-cat." I climbed all the way into the crate and sat there with my legs crossed. It was a pretty big crate, actually. And we'd put a blanket over the metal tray at the bottom so it wasn't too uncomfortable.

Of course, right when I was sitting inside a dog crate had to be the moment when Kristal Perkins walked into the room. She took one look at me and started cracking up.

"Oh — uh — hi, Kristal," I said. I could tell my face was turning bright red. "How did you get in?" Merlin trotted over to her, wagging his tail.

"Your sister let me in," she said. "Why are you inside the crate and the dog's out here? Isn't it supposed to be the other way around?" She laughed again, showing her braces. Usually she smiles with her mouth closed so people won't see them, but I like it when she laughs without thinking about it. Except, of course, when she's laughing at me.

"I'm trying to show Merlin it's not scary in there," I explained, crawling out of the crate. "He won't even go near it."

She knelt down and buried her hands in Merlin's fur, rubbing his back. He licked her face and she laughed again. "Are you a silly dog?" she said to him. "Are you afraid of your own crate? Come on over here, silly." She inched toward the crate and Merlin followed her. But when she got about a foot away from it, he stopped and lay down again, covering his nose with his paws.

"I think I get it," Camellia said, coming back into the room. She tucked her cell phone into her jeans and put the dog book back on the table. "Katie says they put him in his crate whenever he was being bad. He probably associates it with punishment." She shook her head with a sigh. "That's exactly why the book says *not* to do that. Sometimes I think Katie didn't even read any of these books."

"Awww," Kristal said, scratching Merlin's head. "You're not being punished, poor dog, don't worry."

"Let's try leaving the door open and putting some treats inside," Camellia suggested. "Maybe he'll smell them and go in looking for them, and that'll make him feel better about the crate."

I got some of the treats that were shaped like tiny steaks and scattered them around the inside of the crate. But Merlin stayed on the other end of the room, wagging his tail, and then he followed us into the kitchen.

"We'll just leave it like that," Camellia suggested, "and see if he finds them later."

"Are you taking him to the park again?" Kristal asked. She sat down on one of the stools at the kitchen island. "Skye told me she saw you guys yesterday, and I was wondering if you'd let me film Merlin."

"Sure!" I said, impressed. "You have a video camera?" Merlin got up and trotted out of the room. I hoped he was going to search his crate for treats.

"Dad let me borrow his for my art camp projects," she said. "Yesterday was the last day, but I thought making a Merlin movie would still be fun."

"Yeah, that'd be cool," I said.

"Merlin!" Camellia shouted. "Where did you get that?!"

Merlin poked his head around the door. Dangling from his mouth was a pair of girl's underwear.

I don't know who was more embarrassed, me or Camellia or Kristal. Certainly not Merlin — his tail was going a hundred miles an hour.

Camellia dove at him, and he immediately took off. We listened to him run up the stairs with my sister chasing him. I could hear her shouting and feet thumping as they galloped around upstairs. Then we heard him coming back down the stairs, and Kristal and I jumped up to help.

We chased him around the living room and through my dad's study and into the kitchen and around the island and back up the stairs. You'd think three of us would have had more luck catching one dog, but Kristal was laughing so hard she wasn't really much help. And Merlin was really good at dodging when we jumped at him.

By the time we finally cornered him in Camellia's room, I was pretty near convinced that he really did have magical disappearing powers.

Camellia's room was usually superneat and tidy, but today there were open suitcases on the floor and piles of clothes laid out on the bed. I held Merlin while Camellia wrestled her underwear away from him.

"I never thought I'd agree with Katie," she said, "but seriously, *gross*, dog." She dropped it in her laundry hamper. He made a lunge for one of the piles of clothes, and I had to practically wrap myself around him to hold him back.

"I'll take him to the park while you pack," I suggested.

"Great idea," Camellia said, pointing to the door. "Out you go, all of you. And don't come back until all this stuff is in suitcases!"

I dragged Merlin down the stairs, and Kristal followed us. Of course, then she had to watch the mad chaos of me trying to get his leash on him. This was definitely the highest number of embarrassing things that had ever happened to me in front of her. All thanks to Merlin. I knew dogs could be difficult, but embarrassing? Why didn't anyone warn me about that?

CHAPTER 6

We spent the rest of the day at the park with Danny and Eric. Kristal filmed Merlin bounding around the dog run and chasing the tennis ball. She got some great shots of him setting off the water fountain and trying to jump in it. She even videotaped him jumping up to lick the camera lens.

Around dinnertime, Camellia called my cell phone to say it was safe to come home. She still wasn't very pleased with Merlin, though. And nothing I could say would change her mind about putting him in his crate for the night.

"We'll put something in there that smells like you," she said. "That'll make him like it better." She had gotten this idea from one of the books, of course. So I had to go get an old T-shirt and stick it in the crate with the blanket and the treats. Merlin sat up on the couch and watched me do this. He looked pretty suspicious. His long, dangly ears scooted forward on his head and he even stopped smiling for a few seconds.

As soon as I stood up and stepped toward him, Merlin leaped off the couch and went tearing off down the hall.

"Camellia!" I shouted. "Dad! Help me catch him!"

Dad came out of his study, blinking in surprise, and Merlin galloped right into him. Dad tried to reach for his collar, but Merlin scrambled around like lightning and disappeared up the stairs.

"I hope your door is closed," I said to Camellia as she came running out of the kitchen.

"It definitely is!" she said. We chased Merlin up the stairs, but when we got up there, we couldn't find him. He wasn't in the bathroom. He wasn't in Dad's bedroom. He wasn't on my bed. Camellia's door was still closed, but we opened it to double-check. Half her stuff was packed away in suitcases and boxes. It made me sad to look at it. But there was no Merlin in there.

"He *is* a magician!" I said.

"He's a big dog," Dad said. "He didn't just disappear. Let's look again."

We checked all the rooms again more carefully. Finally I spotted a long golden tail sticking out from under my bed. I lay down on the carpet and looked. Merlin's big brown eyes met mine and his tail went *thump thump*. He looked so happy to see me, I felt bad telling on him. But if I didn't, my sister and my dad would keep looking for him all night.

"Come on, boy," I said, holding out my hand. "It's just for the night. Don't worry."

With a small, sad noise, Merlin wriggled forward on his belly a little, but he didn't come all the way out from under the bed. I reached for his collar and tugged on it, but he wouldn't come. Camellia and Dad both tried calling him, too. In the end I had to go downstairs and get some treats. *Those* got him out from under the bed in a hurry.

I held out another treat and led him down the stairs. Chomping happily on the first treat, he followed me. He poked my hand with his shiny black nose. He didn't even notice where we were going until we were standing in the living room.

Then he suddenly planted his feet, staring at the crate. He started to back away, but my dad and Camellia were ready for him. Dad grabbed his collar. I tried to give Merlin the treat, but he wasn't interested anymore. He just wanted to get away. He was wriggling and scrabbling in place. My dad tried to pull him over to the crate, but Merlin was flailing around too much. Camellia ran over and brought the crate to Dad. With a heave, Dad wrestled him inside and closed the door.

"WOOF!" Merlin protested, clawing at the door. "WOOF! WOOF!"

"I'm sorry, buddy," I said, kneeling and poking the treat through the bars. He gobbled it up, giving me this look, like he was thinking *You're not going to bribe me into liking this.* Then he started sniffing around the bottom of the crate, digging up the blanket. He found another of the treats and ate that, too.

"Quick, while he's distracted," Camellia said, turning off the light. We all snuck upstairs and got ready for bed in a hurry. I listened hard while I was brushing my teeth, but all I could hear from downstairs was snuffling and sometimes crunching when he found another treat.

Everything seemed quiet when I got into bed. The house was dark and still. Dad was in his room reading and Camellia was in her room, making lists of last-minute things she needed. I was tired from running around the park. I started to fall asleep right away.

Then I heard a mournful whimper from downstairs. Merlin went "arooo arooo aroooo" a few times and then stopped. I heard the scrabbling of claws on metal. Then I heard *RATTLE CLANK RATTLE CLANK RATTLE CLANK!*

"Merlin!" Camellia said from the top of the stairs. "Shush! No!"

He was quiet again, and she went back into her room.

A long pause. I closed my eyes.

RATTLE RATTLE RATTLE RATTLE RATTLE RATTLE RATTLE.

"Just ignore him," my dad called. "He'll calm down eventually."

Pause.

RATTLE RATTLE RATTLE CLANK CLANK.

More whimpering. More scratching noises.

RATTLE RATTLE. RATTLE RATTLE. CLANK. RATTLE RATTLE.

"Aroooooo. Aaaarrrrrooo."

Pause. Long pause. I began to drift off.

RATTLE RATTLE RATTLE RATTLE CLANK CLANK CLANK RATTLE RATTLE CLANK RATTLE RATTLE CLANK CLANK CLANK . . .

BANG!

I leaped out of bed. Dad and Camellia were already running down the hall from different directions. We nearly crashed into each other at the top of the stairs. Merlin was sitting proudly at the bottom, wagging his tail and grinning.

Camellia gasped. "How did he do that?"

"Let's go see," my dad said, rubbing his forehead.

We all went down to the living room. Merlin came and pressed himself up against me like, *Don't worry, I sorted it out. We'll never be separated again!* I knew I wasn't supposed to pet him, but he was wagging his tail so hard, I couldn't resist scratching behind his ears just a little bit.

The tray at the bottom of the crate had been pushed out and was lying halfway across the room from it. The crate itself was on its side — the bang we heard must have been when it fell over. The blanket and my shirt were scrunched up at one end. And the door was lying open.

Camellia was flabbergasted. "That — that is — I can't — how —"

"I have an idea," Dad said. "Why don't we see if he'll sleep on the floor beside Parker? That way we all might get some peace and quiet."

Merlin and I looked at Camellia hopefully. She

put her hands on her hips. "I'm not sure that's sending the right message," she said, giving Merlin a stern look. "But I guess nothing else is working. . . ."

"I'll be very bossy," I promised. "I'll alpha-dog him right off the bed, I swear."

She sighed. "OK, let's try it."

I dragged Merlin's bed into my room. He was *so* excited to see this. He kept jumping and leaping and pouncing on it and trying to play with me. "No," I said firmly. "Bedtime." Wagging his tail, he came over and bumped my elbow with his nose. I settled his bed on the floor next to mine. "Bed," I said, pointing to it.

He jumped up onto my bed, turned around a few times, and curled up right in the center of the sheets. His tail swished back and forth. His fur puffed out around his legs like a fluffy jacket. He smiled at me like he was saying *OK, sure, you sleep down there, and I'll sleep up here.*

Camellia was watching from the door. "Nope," I said. "You sleep down here." I pointed to his bed.

Merlin flopped his head way over to the side in this *aw, shucks* kind of way. He covered his nose with one paw, then peeked out at me like, *But aren't I so cute?*

"Doesn't matter," I said. "Your bed is down here. Merlin, off."

Heaving the most enormous sigh, Merlin pushed himself slowly to his paws and jumped down to the floor. He sniffed his bed dubiously. He started digging in it with his front paws, rearranging all the folds and wrinkles like I had dropped it all wrong and it needed fixing.

"Good work," Camellia said. "Let's see if he stays there."

"He will," I said.

She closed the door behind her and I got back into bed. Merlin turned around a few hundred times, but at last he flopped down in his bed and rested his head on the furry edge of it. He looked up at me with big brown eyes.

I reached down and rubbed his long white belly fur. "Better than the other options, isn't it?" I said.

He made a sleepy, contented noise. I switched off the bedside lamp. The moonlight from the window made his fur look silvery and pale and mysterious.

"Just like a magic dog," I murmured.

Merlin fell asleep before I did. I know because he snored.

CHAPTER 7

Dad took Camellia to the airport on Saturday. He wanted to go with her all the way to Oberlin, but she said he didn't have to. Camellia is pretty good at taking care of herself, in case you couldn't tell.

She freaked out when she realized she couldn't take all her stuff with her on the plane, though. She threw things around her room for a while trying to decide what to leave behind. She kept yelling things like, "But I *need* my entire collection of Jane Austen books!" and "How am I supposed to survive with only five pairs of pajamas? I mean *seriously*!"

Then Dad's girlfriend Julianne called. She must have heard the panicking in the background. She said, "Why don't I take the rest of Camellia's boxes to the post office and mail them to Oberlin?" I could tell Camellia didn't like saying yes to this. But she couldn't exactly say no either. At least this way she could have as many pajamas as she needed.

Dad and Camellia were already gone when

Julianne rang the doorbell. Merlin flew off the couch, barking and barking. This was the first time Julianne was going to meet our new dog. I wondered if she would be like Katie and think Merlin was gross.

When I opened the front door, Merlin shoved his head past me to get to Julianne. His tail was already flying back and forth, and whapping my legs. Some guard dog. He couldn't even figure out who to scare away.

"Oh my goodness!" Julianne said in a really excited voice. She crouched down and let Merlin sniff her hands. He tried to jump on her and she nearly fell over, but she got to her feet, laughing. "What a great dog, Parker! Leonard told me all about him and I've been just dying to meet him."

One of the things I don't like about Julianne is that she calls my dad Leonard. I guess I don't know what else she's supposed to call him, but it's weird because to me his name is Dad. Another thing that I don't like is that she talks all the time. My dad says he likes that because he's so quiet, but I think it's tiring to do that much listening.

"Golden retrievers are my favorite," Julianne said. "I had one when I was a little girl, but Merlin is even more handsome. Aren't you a good boy? Oh, he's just like you, Parker."

That was a weird thing to say. Normally I try not to encourage her, but I wanted to know what that meant. "Just like me?" I said.

"You know, one of those dogs who's so cool and everybody likes him," she said. I was surprised. I didn't know she thought I was cool. Plus she's wrong about everybody liking me. I can think of plenty of people who don't like me, starting with Avery Lafitte and Eric's sisters. "I mean, so, if you were a dog, you would definitely be a golden retriever. Whereas I'd be something like a Pomeranian, yapping and yapping and yapping all the time." She laughed.

"Which ones are Pomeranians?" I asked.

"They look like little orange balls of fluff with four tiny feet sticking out," she said.

"Maybe if you dyed your hair orange instead of red," I said. Then I wondered if I wasn't supposed to say stuff like that, but she laughed.

"I've thought about that!" she said. "Maybe one day." Her hair is shoulder-length and always messy. She usually keeps it pinned back with a clip so it won't fall in her face while she's painting or sculpting or whatever she does.

"So Camellia's boxes are right in here," I said. I felt like I was betraying Camellia by having a real conversation with Julianne. If Julianne thought she was going to come along and replace my sister, she was wrong. Even if dopey Merlin did like her.

Julianne came in and lifted the top two boxes. "Oof!" she said. "Is she bringing her whole library with her?"

"I think so," I said. I couldn't believe Julianne could carry two of the boxes at once. They were pretty heavy.

I helped her carry the boxes to her car. I blocked Merlin in the kitchen so that we could leave the front door open. I knew he would get through the baby gate, but I figured it would take him a little while.

When we got back from our last trip to the car, Merlin was sitting right inside the door watching us. He wagged his tail.

"Wow!" Julianne said. "He's an escape artist, isn't he?"

"Yeah," I said, scratching his head.

"But it's amazing that he didn't try to run away," Julianne said. "He just wanted to be with us. That's pretty cute, Merlin." She made a gesture to him with one of her hands and he held out his paw for her to shake. "Look how smart you are!" she said, ruffling his neck fur with both her hands.

"I didn't know he could do that," I said.

"If you want any help training him, let me know," Julianne said. "I bet he'd learn really quickly."

"Maybe," I said. I wanted to teach him tricks, but I didn't want to hang out with Julianne. Our family was fine without her.

"Great," she said. "See you later! Thanks for your help with the boxes!"

It was really quiet in the house after she left. Plus it started raining, so I couldn't even take Merlin to the park. Plus I knew I had to go back to school on Monday and I wasn't really excited about that. So Merlin and I lay on the couch and watched TV while we waited for my dad to come home. I put on Animal Planet because Merlin seemed to really like it. He kept cocking his head at the TV every time a dog or a meerkat or a monkey or a polar bear ran across the screen. I didn't know dogs could watch TV, but I think he totally understood what was happening.

When Dad got home, he came in and sat on the couch beside me. He rubbed Merlin's head. "I guess it's just us boys now," he said.

"Yeah," I agreed. I was glad he didn't say "and Julianne."

We sat there for a while watching orangutans try to fish.

"I was thinking," Dad said, "that maybe we should order a Meat Lover's pizza for dinner."

I grinned at him. "That sounds awesome."

Camellia called later that night. She told us all about her roommate and her dorm and the campus and the airplane ride and everything. I couldn't tell if she missed us or if she was too excited about being at college to miss us yet. I held up the phone to Merlin's ear and she yelled, "Hi Merlin!" and he went, "WOOF!" and looked around all startled, trying to figure out where she was.

On Sunday it was still gray and drizzly. We tried leaving Merlin outside in the yard for a while by himself to see if he would escape. He sniffed along the fence and ran in circles for a while, but then he came and sat by the back door and just waited for us to let him back in. So I figured he'd be OK. Our yard was much harder to escape from than Katie's.

Finally it was Monday, and time for school.

And of course it was the most perfect sunny day. Have you ever noticed that? For some reason the first day of school always has the best weather. It's like the sun is trying to torture me.

I put a bowlful of water at either end of the yard for Merlin, in case he accidentally knocked one of them over. I put on my backpack, said good-bye to

Dad, and took Merlin out the back door. He galloped around the yard with his fur flying and swishing around him. At the back of the garden, he found a tennis ball that I'd been throwing for him on Friday. He ran over to me and dropped it at my feet, crouching with his front paws down and his butt up in the air. He waggled his tail, waiting for me to throw it.

"I'm sorry, boy, I can't," I said, patting his head. "I have to go to school. But you hang out here, and I'll come right home afterward."

He picked up the ball and dropped it in front of me again.

"We'll play after school," I said. "I promise." He watched me with his head tilted to one side as I got up and went over to the gate. It's one of those with a latch you lift up to go through. Merlin whimpered sadly as I closed the gate behind me. I made sure the latch was firmly in place. Then I waved good-bye to Merlin and walked up to the corner, where Danny and Eric were waiting for me.

"Poor Merlin!" Eric said, waving to my dog. Merlin had his nose pressed to the chain links and was watching us walk away down the street. It was the saddest thing I'd ever seen.

Danny was on his bike, as always, and he rode up and down and in circles around us as Eric and I walked. Sometimes Troy walks with us, but his mom always likes to drive him on the first day of school . . . or if it's raining . . . or if she thinks it's going to rain . . . or if he sneezed the day before. I shouldn't make fun, though — she usually picks all of us up if it's raining, which is really nice.

We were halfway to school when I heard something like footsteps running behind us. I figured it was another kid until I heard a familiar "WOOF!"

I spun around. "Merlin!"

He skidded to a stop, his tail waving madly. He jumped up and licked my face, then danced in a circle, barking with joy.

"No, no," I said, hooking my fingers in his collar. "You're supposed to stay at home! Bad dog!" He grinned and panted at me like he had no idea what that meant. I pulled out my cell phone and called our house, but Dad had already left for work.

What could I do? I thought about calling Dad's cell phone, but I didn't want to make him late either. He has to be there to open the bank right on time.

Camellia would have known what to do. Actually, I realized, Camellia would have just taken care of it herself.

I shook my head. "I'm going to have to take him back, guys."

"But you'll be late," Eric said, checking his watch.

"I know," I said. "You guys go ahead. Tell Mr. Peary I'm sorry. I have to figure out how he got out."

Danny and Eric exchanged looks. "I'll come with you," Danny said. "Maybe if I ride ahead I can figure it out before you get there."

"And I'll go on and tell the teachers what happened," Eric said. "Mr. Peary will understand."

I hoped that was true. I didn't know much about my new teacher, but he seemed kind of strict. Teachers usually like Eric, though, because he's quiet and gets good grades, so he seemed like the best messenger.

"Thanks, you guys," I said. "Come on, Merlin, let's go!" I started running home and Merlin ran along beside me. His ears flapped back in the wind and his paws skimmed the sidewalk. It would have been a great feeling if I weren't panicking about being late for the first day of sixth grade.

Danny pedaled ahead, so by the time we got back to my house, he'd already dumped his bike on the grass. He was standing by the gate to the backyard, which was wide open.

"I think he opened the gate," Danny said.

"Boy, I'm glad you went on ahead to figure that out," I said.

"Shut up, I'm helping," he said. "Look, he must have lifted the latch. Do you think he could do that?"

"He can do anything," I said, shaking my head. "But maybe I left it unlatched by accident. Let's put him back inside and you watch to see what he does. I'll go look in the garage — maybe there's something in there we can use to lock it."

I ran to the garage. My heart was pounding. School was supposed to start in a few minutes. Even if I ran all the way there, I'd miss the first bell. And I hadn't even figured out what to do with Merlin yet.

I went to my dad's tool bench and picked up a coil of white string. Maybe I could tie the gate shut. But a lock would be better. I started digging through the piles of stuff — screwdrivers, nails, tape measures. . . .

Danny appeared in the door of the garage, breathless. Merlin was right behind him. He didn't know what we were all excited about, but he was happy to be excited, too. He bounced on his front paws and barked and danced in circles.

"That was wild!" Danny said. "As soon as you disappeared, he went straight to the gate and lifted the latch with his nose. He didn't even care that I was right there watching him!"

"You dork," I said to Merlin. "If I get detention for being tardy, I won't be able to come home and play with you. Think about that!"

He wagged his tail. I don't think he was thinking very hard.

"There!" I said, spotting an old bike lock lying on a shelf. Luckily the key was still in the padlock. I grabbed it and we ran back out to the yard. Merlin raced right through the open gateway and over to his tennis ball. He picked it up and threw it in the air. Then he turned to look at me, asking me to come play with him.

"Sorry, Merlin!" I called as we pushed the gate shut. I started winding the bike chain through the links of the fence and the gate. Merlin came over and sniffed at my hands as I worked. He stretched up and nosed at the latch, but Danny held the gate shut so he couldn't come out.

I snapped the lock into place, stood up, and put the key in my pocket. Danny lifted the latch and tried to push the gate open. It stayed where it was. There wasn't even a small gap for a dog to squeeze through. I wagged my finger at Merlin.

"No more tricks, wizard dog," I said. "Stay!"

Merlin whined and pawed at the gate.

"Come on," Danny said. "We gotta go."

"You go ahead," I said. "Don't be late because of me." I ran to grab my bike and helmet from the garage. Maybe if I pedaled fast I could still make it.

I could see Danny a few blocks ahead of me as I swung out of my driveway. I pumped hard on the pedals, standing up on the bike. The wind whooshed past. I was glad the streets were so empty. But the emptier they were close to the school, the later I knew I was. I thought I heard the first bell ring as I came around the last corner. There was no one on the school steps or on the front lawn.

I flew into the school parking lot and shoved my bike into the bike racks. I hung my helmet on the handlebars and tried to fix my hair as I hurried up the front steps.

The second bell rang.

The school door opened. Vice Principal Taney was standing there looking at me.

"Nice of you to join us, Mr. Green," he said. He always calls us "Mr." this and "Ms." that. I think that's because he knows it scares the heck out of us. "You are late. Come to my office."

The first day of school, and I was already in trouble, thanks to Merlin.

CHAPTER 8

Vice Principal Taney is a tall, bony guy with very white hair. He has permanent wrinkles in his forehead from frowning so much. His nose is long and pointy. We're all pretty sure he doesn't like kids at all. He usually walks around the halls looking for ways to get people in trouble.

"I'm sorry, Mr. Taney," I said, following him into the school office. The receptionist, Adele, looked up and smiled at me. "It was an accident — I can explain."

"That's what they always say," Mr. Taney said, pulling a detention pad out of his jacket.

A tall African-American woman came out of the principal's office in the back. She had long black braids tied back with a peach-colored scarf. I'd never seen her before, but I guessed she was meeting with Principal Ernst. She paused at the mailbox outside the office, looking through a stack of papers.

"It was my dog," I said. "He got loose and followed me and I had to take him home and make sure he couldn't get out again."

Mr. Taney was already starting to write the detention slip. His eyebrows were raised up high like he didn't believe me.

"What kind of dog?" the strange woman asked curiously.

"He's a golden retriever," I said. "We just got him."

"I have this under control, Mrs. Hansberry," Vice Principal Taney said.

"Well, it sounds like a reasonable excuse to me," said the woman. She put her pile of papers on the front desk and held out her hand to me. "And you are?"

"Parker Green, ma'am," I said, shaking her hand. I wanted to ask who she was, but I thought it would be impolite. Luckily she just went ahead and told me.

"I'm Mrs. Hansberry, your new principal," she said. "And lucky for you, I have a misbehaving dog myself. Mr. Taney, I think we can make an exception on the first day."

Mr. Taney's lips were pressed together into very thin lines. "Certainly," he said in a tight voice.

Principal Hansberry wrote something on a slip of paper and handed it to me. "Give that to your teacher," she said. "Whose class are you in?"

"Sixth grade, Mr. Peary," I said. There were two other sixth grade classes. Troy was in Miss Woodhull's and Hugo was in Mr. Guare's, but luckily Danny and Eric were both in the same class as me.

"All right, hurry along," she said. "Try not to let it happen again."

I wanted to run all the way down the hall, but I knew Vice Principal Taney was still watching. He'd probably give me a detention for that too. So I just walked as fast as I could.

When I pulled open the door to Mr. Peary's class, I saw that everyone was pushing their desks around. Eric and Danny both looked super-relieved to see me.

I handed Mrs. Hansberry's note to the teacher. Mr. Peary isn't nearly as old as Mr. Guare. He only graduated from college a few years ago. He has brown hair and kind of a thin scruffy beard. Camellia said once she thought he was trying to grow facial hair to make himself look older. I think the stern look on his face made him look plenty old enough.

But he nodded when he saw the note. "Eric told me what happened," he said. "Grab a desk, Parker. We're arranging them in a semicircle."

This was something new. We'd always sat in rows in all our other classrooms. But with Mr. Peary directing, we got the desks all set up like three sides of a square. On the open side was his desk and the blackboard. There was a space in the middle where he stood to talk to us.

I managed to shove my desk in beside Danny's. Eric was on his other side. Rebekah Waters sat next to Eric, which I knew would make him really nervous. Eric is kind of shy, except with us, and he thinks Rebekah is the prettiest girl in the class. So he definitely, definitely can't talk to her.

Rebekah is cute, for sure, but if you asked me, I'd say Natasha Kandinsky is prettier. She'd gotten new glasses over the summer with thin silver rims that made her look like a high schooler. She has masses of black hair, all the way down to her waist. But she's one of the silliest girls I've ever met. Natasha spends every recess sitting on the wall and giggling with her best friend, Tara Washington. It's totally impossible to talk to them, because they'll just start giggling and you never have any idea what is supposed to be so funny.

She was sitting across the classroom, next to Tara, of course. They were already whispering to each other, even though I was sure they'd spent the whole summer together. Kristal was sitting on the other side of Tara, and she waved hi to me. Which of course made Tara and Natasha whisper and giggle even more.

Nikos Stavros took the other desk next to me. He's really smart, and he usually reads instead of playing baseball or whatever the rest of us are playing. But watch out if he asks you over to play video games — he beats everyone at everything, hands down.

"All right," Mr. Peary said, sitting on top of his desk to face us. "Let's go around the room and introduce ourselves. Tell us your name and something interesting about yourself."

I am so bad at this game. Ms. Applebaum made us do the same thing, and I could never think of anything interesting to say. I'm just a regular guy. I think last year I said something like, "I like baseball" or "My favorite fruit is blueberries." I know, *so* fascinating.

Ella Finegold was first. She stood up and said, "I'm Ella, and this summer I learned two new solos on the piano. I haven't decided which one I'm going to do for the talent show yet." She sat back down. I saw Tara and Natasha rolling their eyes at each other. Ella is a total musical genius, but she sang some kind of slow opera thing at last year's fall talent show, and everyone nearly fell asleep.

When it was my turn, I said, "I'm Parker, and . . . I have a new dog." Thinking about Merlin made me smile as I sat back down.

"What kind of dog?" Nikos asked.

"A golden retriever," I said. "His name is Merlin."

"Oh, wow!" Heidi Tyler said. "That is so cool! I love dogs! I want one so badly!"

"He's the most handsome dog ever," Kristal said. I was glad she didn't say "gorgeous."

"Does he look anything like that dog out there?" Natasha asked, pointing out the window.

I turned to look out at the playground.

Merlin was sitting under the slide, wagging his tail and wearing the biggest grin I'd ever seen.

CHAPTER 9

I stood up so fast my chair fell over.

"That's my dog!" I said.

"Oooooh, he's beautiful," said Rebekah. She got up and leaned on the windowsill. Almost everyone else in the class came crowding around to stare at my dog. Only Ella stayed in her seat like she wasn't interested. Tara and Natasha started giggling. Now I could see other kids looking out of other windows around the playground. Everyone was pointing at Merlin.

"Can I go get him, please, Mr. Peary?" I asked. My face was burning bright red. I didn't know what to do. I just knew I had to get out of there — and I had to get Merlin out of there.

Mr. Peary looked confused, too. He rubbed his beard. "Let me call the principal's office," he said, going around to the other side of his desk.

My stomach felt like it had a big hole in it. I hated being in trouble. I didn't like having everyone staring at me. And I was worried about Merlin. It wasn't safe for him to run around in the streets like that, even though there is so little traffic in our neighborhood.

"Look at him just sitting there," Tara marveled. "My dog can't sit still for thirty seconds."

"What kind of dog do you have?" Danny asked.

"Bananas is a Boston terrier," Tara said. "He's totally insane."

"At least he's never followed you to school," I said.

"Oh, I want a dog SO MUCH!" Heidi said. Heidi is the tallest girl in our class. She's one of the ones who is easy to talk to, like Kristal. "Parker, if he stays for recess, can I pet him?"

"He can't stay until recess!" I said. "He's supposed to be at home!"

"I want a dog too," Danny said to Heidi.

"No way, cats are much better," Maggie Olmstead said. Her cat is in all these cat food commercials. Everyone knows that because she talks about it all the time. I wondered if having a famous cat was better than having a dog. You couldn't run around in the park with a cat. But then, a cat probably wouldn't show up at school and massively embarrass you and maybe get you suspended by the new principal on the first day of sixth grade.

"Parker," Mr. Peary said, "Mrs. Hansberry says to get your dog and take him to her office."

"Ooooooooooohhhhh," said some of the guys in the class.

"Yes, Mr. Peary," I said.

Now I had to go out there with practically everyone in the whole school watching. I ran down the hall to the big door that goes outside. I stopped for a minute, taking deep breaths. From here I could see all the windows that face the playground. I could see lots and lots of faces looking out. I wished the fire alarm would go off and distract everyone, but of course it didn't.

I opened the door to the playground.

Merlin leaped to his feet when he saw me. His tail was going about a million miles an hour. He barked and ran in a circle around the slide. He kept turning to look at me.

"Come here, boy," I said, crouching and holding out my hand to him.

He came part of the way toward me and then ran back to the slide. I saw that he had found a lost sneaker somewhere. He picked it up and looked at me, wagging his tail. The shoe stuck out of the sides of his mouth and made him look really goofy. It didn't look like one of mine. I wondered whose it was. I was sort of afraid to find out. He'd probably stolen it from the kindergarten cubbies.

Well, it could be a lot worse, I thought, remembering the Camellia packing fiasco.

"Come on, Merlin," I said, walking toward him.

"Mmmoorf," he mumble-barked around the shoe. I was nearly close enough to grab him when he suddenly took off, racing around the slide and away behind the swings. He stopped and sat down, dropping the shoe.

I ran after him. He gleefully picked up the shoe and went galloping off to the seesaw.

Oh, no. No, I was not going to chase my dog around the playground with the whole school watching.

But what else could I do? The only thing I was sure would work was treats, and I didn't have any of those.

On the other hand, Merlin didn't know that.

I put my hand in my pocket and pretended to pull something out. Keeping my hand closed, I held it out to him. "Mmmm," I said. "Yummy . . . um, steak-shaped things. You know you want them."

Merlin's ears scooted forward. He tilted his head, watching my hand. I backed away, still holding it out. "Come on, Merlin," I called.

He trotted toward me a few steps. Then he turned, remembering the shoe, and bent his head to sniff at it. He looked at me. I took another step back.

His love of food won out. He came running over to me and jumped up to put his front paws on my chest. I hooked my fingers in his collar and he licked my hand all over, clearly wondering where his treat had disappeared to.

I heard clapping coming from some of the windows. Danny yelled, "Woo hoo!" and I saw Mr. Peary trying to herd everyone back to their seats. With my face on fire, I tugged Merlin into the school with me.

He trotted next to me, just happy to be there, but I kept a firm grip on his collar anyway. Vice Principal Taney was standing outside the administration office as we came up. He gave Merlin the look he usually saves for little kids who sneeze on him. But he didn't say anything as I opened the door and herded Merlin inside.

"Oh, honey," Adele said, standing up to see over the counter. "He *is* a darling."

"Not today he isn't," I said.

Principal Hansberry opened the door to her office. Merlin bounded over and started sniffing her pant legs. She laughed and petted him.

"He can probably smell my dog," she said.

"I'm really, really sorry about this, Principal Hansberry," I said. "We locked him in the yard — I don't know how he got out."

"I'm sure it's not your fault," she said. "These things happen. But I'm afraid we can't have him disrupting the school day." She went behind her desk and sat down. I followed her into her office, feeling nervous. Merlin trotted over to her bookcase and started nosing books around as if he was deciding which one to read next.

"I could run him home," I said. "I only live a few blocks away."

She shook her head. "I'd rather not have you off school grounds during school hours. Don't worry, I've called your father."

I winced. "Oh, man. What did he say?"

"He said he was afraid of something like this," she said with a smile. "He's coming right over to get him."

"Merlin," I said, sitting down with a sigh. "Why do you have to cause so much trouble?" Merlin came over, put his paws up on my lap, and licked my face.

"You said this is a new dog, right?" Mrs. Hansberry said. I nodded. "Sometimes it can take a while to figure out the best thing to do with them during the day."

"What do you do?" I asked.

She opened a drawer and pushed a few things around until she found a business card. She pulled it out and handed it to me. "I leave her at this day care center."

"Day care for dogs?" I said. I'd never heard of that.

"It's pretty affordable," she said. "They walk them for you, and it's a chance for your dog to spend time with other dogs, too. See what your dad thinks."

I heard the front door of the office open. Merlin sat up and went, "Woof!" My dad came hurrying in.

"I'm sorry, Dad," I said quickly. "I padlocked the gate, but he must have gotten out some other way."

"I know. We'll figure it out," Dad said. He smiled at Mrs. Hansberry. "Welcome to the school. I bet this isn't what you envisioned for your first day."

"As first-day problems go, I'll definitely take this one," she said, shaking his hand. "At least it's wearing a smile."

That was true. Merlin couldn't seem to *stop* smiling. It was like he'd won the lottery, managing to get me and Dad in one place in the middle of the day.

I told Dad about the day care and showed him the card.

"What kind of dog do you have?" Dad asked her.

"A mutt, through and through," she said. "My husband calls her a Frankendog."

"My ex-wife never liked dogs," Dad said. That was something I didn't know about Mom. But I didn't really know anything about Mom. "So this is our first," he added.

"Well, good luck with him. Now Parker should go back to class," she said.

"Yeah," I said. That was probably the most I'd ever wanted to get back into a classroom.

"I'll put Merlin inside the house for now," Dad said. "I'll slip home later on to let him out. And I'll give this place a call about tomorrow." He held up the card.

"Thanks, Dad," I said with relief. I was glad Merlin wasn't going to be my problem for a few hours, anyway.

"Nice to meet you, Mrs. Hansberry," Dad said, shaking her hand again.

"You too, Mr. Green," she said.

Dad took Merlin's collar and led him out into the hall. When Merlin realized that I was going in a different direction from them, he tried to pull away and follow me. He bounced and slid on his paws, trying to sit down and stop my dad. But Dad kept walking. Merlin gave in and let himself be dragged away. He twisted around to look back at me a few times. I wished I didn't have to go to class. I wished I could go running outside with Merlin.

Instead, I turned and headed down the hall to Mr. Peary's classroom.

CHAPTER 10

When I got to the cafeteria at lunchtime, I could feel everyone staring at me. I kept hearing the word "dog" as I passed by the tables. All the kids in classrooms that faced the playground were telling everyone else about Merlin. I was so embarrassed, I think even the tips of my ears were red.

Eric could tell that I didn't want to talk about it. Eric is good at noticing that stuff because he's pretty quiet, too. But Danny thought it was the funniest thing that had ever happened at our school, so he went on and on and on about it. And Troy came hurrying over to our table as soon as we sat down.

"So how did he get out?" he asked without even saying hi. "Do you know? Have you figured it out?" He sat down and pulled out the brown-bag lunch his mom always packs for him.

"I seriously have no idea," I said.

"It's crazy!" Danny said. "We locked the gate!

There's no way he could have gotten it open. And Parker's fence is so high! It's practically as tall as me!"

"Maybe he dug a hole?" Troy suggested.

"He didn't look all dirty," I said. "And I think it would have taken him longer than that."

"You named him after the wrong magician," Eric said. "He's not a Merlin — he's a Houdini!" Eric has read nearly every book there is on Harry Houdini. His parents bought him a magic set last Christmas. The rest of us were bored of card tricks by February, but Eric is still really into illusions and stuff like that.

"We're going to figure this out," Troy said. "We'll stake out your place and watch him until we see what he's doing."

"OK, if you want," I said. "But tomorrow we're taking him to day care, so it won't be a problem anymore."

A tray hit the table beside me. To my surprise, it was Heidi Tyler. The girls had been sitting at a different table from the boys since, like, second grade, so this was really weird. Across the table, Kristal slid in beside Danny. And then Rebekah Waters sat down next to Eric. Eric started paying really close attention to his mashed potatoes. I knew we weren't going to hear another word out of him as long as she was there.

"Oh my goodness," Heidi said right away, "Parker, your dog is the most amazing, fantastic, beautiful thing I've ever seen."

"Yeah," I said. "He's a pain in the butt, though."

"He's not that bad," Kristal said, hiding her smile behind her hand.

"I've been asking my mom for a dog for years and years and *years*," Heidi said. "But she thinks they're too messy."

"They're not too messy," Rebekah said. "Not if you get a little one."

"I'd step on a little dog if I had one," Danny said. Rebekah looked offended, and he added quickly, "I mean, by accident! By accident! Just because I'd be running around and I wouldn't see it there or something."

"Oh, no, that would totally happen to me, too!" Heidi said. In her case, she might be right. If there was a prize for Most Clumsy, Heidi would definitely win. Once last year, she accidentally knocked over the terrarium in Ms. Applebaum's class, and we spent the whole rest of the day chasing down beetles and earthworms and salamanders.

"Heidi and I will have to get big dogs like yours," Danny said to me.

"What about you?" Rebekah said to Eric. "You wouldn't mind a little dog, right?"

Eric looked flustered and started tearing apart his napkin. "Yeah — I mean — no — sure — I'm — cookies," he said suddenly, jumping up and hurrying off to the vending machine.

"Well, tell me if you ever need a dogsitter," Heidi said to me, poking my arm. "I would love, love, *love* to hang out with your dog. And I promise I'd take really good care of him."

"Great. What are you doing from seven a.m. to three p.m. Monday through Friday?" I joked.

"Stupid school," Heidi said with a sigh. She started to put her elbows on the table and her chin on her hands. But her elbow hit her tray, which flew up into the air, scattering chicken nuggets and soggy green beans everywhere. Her milk crashed to the table and sprayed all over Danny and Kristal.

"Oh, no!" Heidi cried, horrified. "I'm so sorry!" She ran off to get napkins.

"Oh, Heidi," Kristal said, but she said it in a nice way. She dabbed at her shirt with one of her napkins. I saw Ella Finegold watching us from one of the corner tables. She usually eats by herself as fast as she can, and then goes to practice piano in the music room while no one else is in there.

"Jeez, I don't know if I'd leave Heidi alone with your dog," Danny joked. Heidi came hurrying back and we cleaned up the table. Then Kristal and Rebekah shared their lunches with Heidi, who kept shaking her head and going, "I'm such a klutz."

It made me feel a lot better, though. At least I wasn't the only person who had an embarrassing first day.

After school, Danny and Troy came home with me. I was a little worried that Merlin might have torn the house apart while we were gone. But when we walked in, he was sitting by the front door, wagging his tail innocently. I guessed maybe he had just slept on the couch all day. He was *so* excited to see us. He jumped up on each of us, barking and bouncing around. He kept running to the back door and back to me.

"All right," Troy said, trying to sound like a police inspector. "Let's solve this case."

I opened the back door, and Merlin shot out into the yard. By the time we got outside he was already back with the tennis ball. He flung it into the air in front of me.

"Let's see," Troy said. He studied my yard. "One of us can watch from the kitchen window. Parker, that should be you, so he can't see you."

"I'll hide up in that tree over there," Danny offered, pointing to a tree outside the fence.

"Good idea," Troy said. "I'll go around the other side of the house, in case he goes that way. Nobody move. We'll watch him until he escapes. Then we'll know how he does it!"

I unlocked the gate so Danny and Troy could get out. Then I wrapped the bike lock chain around it again. Merlin watched me curiously. He trotted up to the fence and pressed his nose to the links, watching Danny climb the tree.

He turned around when he heard Troy running up our neighbor's driveway. Troy peeked around the edge. Merlin bounded over to that corner of the yard and tried to stick his nose through the fence so he could lick Troy's face. Troy went, "EEYURGH!" and hid around the corner again.

I went back inside and stood at the kitchen window. I tried to stay far enough back so Merlin couldn't see me. But our plan didn't work very well. Merlin ran in a circle around the yard. He stopped at the far end and barked at Danny up in the tree. He trotted to the corner and barked at Troy hiding around the side of the house. Then he came to the back door and pawed at it. It was like he was trying to say, *This game is stupid. Let's go to the park! Let's throw tennis balls! Let's chase Frisbees! I haven't seen you all day! Play with me! Play with me!*

I kind of agreed with him. I was sure we wouldn't have to worry anymore once he started day care the next day. But I played along for Troy. I waited almost ten whole minutes. But Merlin didn't try to go anywhere. He finally lay down at the back door and whined sadly.

I gave up and opened the door. Merlin leaped to his feet, smiling his big smile. His long golden fur glowed in the sunshine.

"This isn't working, guys," I called. "Let's just go to the park."

Danny swung down from the tree. "I'm so glad you said that," he said. "My butt was going numb."

"We shouldn't give up yet!" Troy said, sticking his head out.

"Maybe we can try again later," I said. "But seriously, it's no big deal. After tomorrow, it won't be a problem anymore."

But as it turned out, I was completely, totally wrong about that.

CHAPTER 11

Dad and I got up really early on Tuesday morning so we could drive Merlin to day care. We had to bring a whole stack of papers to prove that Merlin had had all his shots. I looked at everything Katie had given us. It seemed like a lot of shots to me. Poor Merlin. But he was all up-to-date. And he was a good dog (well . . . most of the time), so I hoped he would fit in at day care.

The woman on the phone said that there should be no problems, especially with a reference from Mrs. Hansberry. I guess the principal had called them about Merlin. Already I liked her better than Principal Ernst.

Bark and Ride Day Care was in a long brick building off Main Street. We rang the bell and heard barking from inside. Merlin perked up his ears and stopped panting. He looked up at me with his big, trusting brown eyes. It made me feel so guilty about leaving him there.

But I felt better once we went inside and saw how nice it was. The woman in the front office had long blond hair tied back in a ponytail. Her name was Alicia, and her smile was almost as friendly as Merlin's. She let Merlin sniff her hand and then she crouched in front of him to pet him. She said, "Who's this good boy? Are we going to have fun today?" He wagged his tail, and that made me feel better, too.

Alicia took us on a tour. She showed us the big open room where the dogs played when they were let out of their cages. The floor was a rubbery gray material that felt springy under my sneakers. She said they let the dogs play in small groups, so there weren't too many dogs loose at once. Some of the small dogs were nervous of the big dogs, so they got a separate playtime.

"We never let them all out at once. It's easier to manage such a big group that way," Alicia said. Merlin leaned on the end of his leash, trying to drag me over to a small black dog that was sitting placidly in her cage. She blinked at him like she had no idea why he was so excited.

The play area was behind a glass window. That way someone could stand in the front office and watch the dogs playing on the other side. Around the play area, the walls were lined with big, roomy cages. Rainbow-colored paw prints and words like "WOOF!" and "Bow WOW!" were printed on the white walls. Which I'm sure the dogs really appreciated.

"This is where we put the dogs for mealtime, napping, and rest breaks," Alicia said, opening the door of an empty cage. "We give them all a couple of hours to sleep in the afternoon, when they're tired from playing. As you can see, there's plenty of room and a little bed for each of them. If you want, it helps to leave something that smells like you."

Camellia had suggested the same thing on the phone the night before. In my backpack I had the T-shirt we'd tried to put in his crate. Alicia tucked it into the bed in the cage. "There you go, boy," she said to Merlin. He trotted inside and sniffed it dubiously. He started sniffing around the corners of the cage.

Casually, Alicia motioned us out and then closed the door. I was relieved to see that it did not have a doorknob like our bathroom door. It didn't look like the latch on my gate or the door of his crate either. This had a proper bolt that slid across and then clicked down.

I hoped Merlin wouldn't be able to figure this one out. But even if he did, he would still be inside the day care center. They could put him back in the cage. There was no way he could show up at school to surprise me. We were helping him to be a good dog.

Merlin trotted up to the door and poked at the mesh wire with his nose. He peered through it at me, his head drooping.

"Sorry, Merlin," I said. "We'll be back soon." Troy's mom had agreed to drive me over to pick up Merlin after school. She wouldn't be able to do that every day, but we would figure that out later.

As we went back to the front office, I heard Merlin whining and pawing at his door. I felt really sad about leaving him there, but I hoped he would have fun with the other dogs. It sounded a lot more exciting than lying on our couch all day, waiting for me to come home. I kind of wished I could stay and play with all the dogs, too.

Dad was filling out the last form when the front door opened and Principal Hansberry came in with her dog.

"Oh, hello," she said with a smile. "I hoped I'd see you two here." Her dog wagged its tail and stretched out toward me. I held out my hand for it to sniff.

"Hi, Principal Hansberry," I said. "What's your dog's name?"

"This is Luna," she said. She looked a little

embarrassed. "I named her after my favorite Harry Potter character," she admitted.

Luna did look like she was made of lots of different dogs. Her fur was patches of brown and white and black. One ear stood up and the other flopped over. Her tail stuck straight out and her paws looked too big for the rest of her. She had a really cute scruffy face and a little tangled beard under her chin. She was smaller than Merlin, maybe the size of a beagle.

I patted Luna while Dad and Mrs. Hansberry talked. Luna was a lot wrigglier than Merlin. She liked to climb over my legs and around my arms while I was patting her. I wondered if she and Merlin would be friends. Was that weird, if your dog was friends with the principal's dog?

"All right, Parker, let's get you to school on time today," said Dad. "Nice to see you again, Mrs. Hansberry."

"You too," she said.

As we walked back to the car, Dad said, "I'm afraid I have a lot of meetings today, Parker. So if you have any trouble like yesterday, give Julianne a call." He pulled out one of his business cards and wrote her number on the back.

Yeah, right. There were about a hundred people I would call before I would ever call Julianne. I'd rather make Camellia come all the way home from Ohio. I'd rather get beaten up by Avery Lafitte. But I took the card without saying anything.

The only bad thing that happened at school that day was that Avery Lafitte decided to talk to me. Avery is pretty much a big jerk. I'm really glad he's in Mr. Guare's class this year. He loves making other kids cry. He's done that to almost half our class in the last five years. I know he made fun of Ella after her talent show song last year and that made her cry. He always makes fun of Maggie for her famous cat, too, and she hates that.

But I don't let him get to me. At least, I don't show him that he does.

"Parker Green," he said, sitting down at our table and stealing one of Eric's fries. "Where's your dog today, huh? Picking you up after school?"

"Yup," I said. I've figured out that it annoys him when I just agree with him.

"Aw, poor Parker," Avery teased. His eyes were all small and squinty and mean. "He can't be away from his wittle puppy or he misses him, awww."

"Yup," I said. "You got it."

Avery opened his mouth to say something else, but Heidi interrupted him. Yeah, Heidi and Kristal were sitting with us again. It's funny, because if it were Tara and Natasha, I would think maybe they liked one of us. But I got the feeling Heidi liked dogs more than boys. All she wanted to talk about was Merlin. Which was OK by me.

Now she said: "Shut up, Avery. You wish anyone liked you as much as that dog likes Parker." Heidi is another person who never cries when Avery makes fun of her.

Avery's mouth snapped shut. He turned all red and mad-looking. He shoved his chair away from the table and stomped off.

"Nice," Danny said. Kristal grinned, but Heidi shrugged and went back to asking questions about Merlin.

After school, Mrs. Morris was waiting outside in her station wagon. Troy's little sister, Eden, was already in the car. Troy and I got in and waved good-bye to Danny and Eric.

"I can't wait to meet this dog," Troy's mom said. "Troy has talked about nothing else all week."

"Me too!" Eden said. "I want to meet the dog, too!" She's seven with wild dark hair, and she laughs all the time. I've never seen her not smiling.

"He's pretty awesome," I said. "Except when he's bad. But I know he doesn't mean to be."

As we drove to Bark and Ride, I suddenly had a

bad feeling. I was sure something had gone wrong. The moment the car stopped, I jumped out and ran up to the door. Inside I could hear barking — a lot of barking.

I pushed open the door. There was no one in the front office. The phone was ringing and ringing. Papers were scattered around like someone had jumped up in a hurry.

I looked through the big window into the play area.

Dogs were running everywhere!

Every single cage was open and empty. All the dogs were loose. There were small dogs chasing each other in circles. There were big dogs running back and forth from wall to wall. There were medium-sized dogs wrestling each other for toys. One tiny Yorkie was dashing around the room, darting between other dogs' legs, yipping and yipping. A German shepherd had found a toy shaped like a bear and was ripping the stuffing out of it. Bits of white fluff were scattered at his feet. He growled whenever other dogs came near him.

And right in the middle of it all was Merlin. He had dragged his bed out into the play area. He was sitting on top of my T-shirt. He was panting and watching all the dogs with his big, happy smile.

I spotted Luna rolling around with the little black dog I'd seen that morning. They both looked like they were having a wonderful time.

Alicia and her two assistants, on the other hand, were not having a wonderful time at all. They were trying to catch the dogs. They looked really frazzled. Alicia grabbed a big black Newfoundland's collar. She stuck a treat in front of his nose and he followed it back into his cage. She threw a treat into the next cage. A shaggy, long-legged gray dog chased it inside and Alicia quickly shut the door.

One of her assistants managed to corner the Yorkie. He scooped up the tiny dog and put her in a cage. The Yorkie jumped up against the wire mesh. I couldn't believe how high she could jump. She nearly reached the door handle, springing up and down like she was on a trampoline. She was still yapping as loud as she could.

Troy and Eden and their mom came in behind me.

"Whoa," Troy said, looking through the window. "Mass craziness!"

"Look at all the happy dogs!" Eden squealed.

"That's not supposed to happen," I said.

"Don't worry," Troy's mom said. "I'm sure they have everything under control."

We watched Alicia lead a few more big dogs back into their cages. While she was busy with a Great Dane, I saw Merlin get up and trot over to the door that led to the front office. He glanced back at the day care people. They were too busy to notice what he was doing. He sniffed around the edges of the door. He sniffed at the doorknob. He scrabbled at the bottom of the door.

And then he stood up on his back paws and wrapped his front paws around the doorknob. On the other side, we all saw the knob start to turn. I gasped. So that was how he got out of the bathroom!

"Merlin!" Alicia shouted. He dropped to all four paws and sprang away from the door immediately. He gave Alicia an innocent look like, *Who, me? Nothing! Nothing going on here!*

"Merlin, come here," she said firmly. He trotted over to her and she clipped a leash onto him. "You're coming where we can keep an eye on you," she said, shaking her finger at him. She led him across the floor to the office. The other two were still busy chasing down the last few dogs.

Merlin's tail started wagging as soon as he saw us. He tried to jump toward me, but Alicia held him back. "Down, boy," she said, and he sat down, looking up at her for permission.

"Hi Alicia," I said nervously. I introduced Troy's family. "So, um . . . how'd it go?"

"Well, as you saw, we had a bit of a situation," Alicia said. Her hair was falling out of its ponytail and she pushed it back off her forehead.

"What happened?" I asked.

"I'm not sure. I'd put all the dogs in their cages for the afternoon nap," she said. "And I was doing paper-work out here, so I didn't see it start. But I have a pretty good idea." She gave Merlin a stern look. "I want to check the tapes to be sure."

Troy lit up. That sounded like a line straight out of one of his favorite cop shows. "Tapes?" he said eagerly. "What tapes?"

"We have a camera on the dogs all the time," Alicia said, pointing to a TV monitor at the back of the room. "Just in case." She led the way to the monitor and hit the Rewind button. We saw all the dogs running around in reverse. It zipped back to the point where they were all in their cages again. Then she hit Play.

Most of the dogs were lying in their beds, sleep-ing. A couple of them were trotting around their cages or scratching themselves. But one was at the door to his cage, poking at the bolt with his paw.

Merlin. Of course.

He pawed and pawed at the bolt. Then he shoved at the wire with his nose. The bolt lifted up off the ring it sat on. Merlin started pawing at it again, and slowly the bolt slid back and back and back. Sometimes he used his teeth or his nose. He was very patient. *Paw paw paw paw paw poke poke nose nose paw paw.* Soon he had the bolt shoved all the way back. He leaned into the mesh and his door swung open slowly.

The dogs in the cages on either side of him sat up. A Dalmatian came to the front of his cage and pawed at the wire, whining a little. Merlin trotted over to him and stopped. He was nose to nose with the dog inside. His tail wagged. They looked like they were telling each other deep secrets. After a moment, he scampered over to the door and began pawing at that lock. Now that he had figured out how to work it, it took him no time at all to get the lock undone.

That door was still swinging open as Merlin trotted happily on to the next cage. The Dalmatian squeezed through as soon as he could and ran across the room to grab a toy. I couldn't even believe it. It was like a movie about a prison break. We watched as Merlin went down the whole row, opening one cage after another. Behind him, dogs began to come out of their cages. Some of them were cautious, sniffing at their doors as they moved. Some of them kept sleeping at first. But some of them came bounding out as soon as they could get free.

Alicia paused the tape. "Oh, dear," she said. She rubbed the sides of her head.

"I didn't know he could do that," I said. "I'm really, really sorry. Merlin, you are such a bad dog!" Merlin looked up at me and wagged his tail. His face was sweet and open, like always. He had no idea how much trouble he was causing. He just wanted to play with all those dogs. He never meant to cause total chaos.

Alicia was really nice about it, but she said Merlin couldn't come back to day care. They had to worry about the other dogs. It wasn't safe to have an escape artist running around loose — especially one who liked to open all the other cages, too! I could understand that. And she didn't charge us for that day, even though they had had to do so much extra work because of him.

So that was the end of that plan. Now I had no idea what we were going to do.

CHAPTER 12

"It's OK," Troy said as we all got into his mom's car. "I have the best idea!"

"Oh, good," I said. "Because I have no ideas at all." Merlin lay down and put his head on my lap. His tail thumped against Troy's jeans. He kept looking up as if he was checking that I was still there. In the front seat, Eden couldn't stop wriggling around to look at him. The smile on her face was almost as big as Merlin's.

"We do what the day care place does," Troy said. "We use a camera and secretly tape him breaking out of your yard. Then we'll know how he's getting out, so we can stop him!"

That did sound pretty smart. "Kristal has a video camera," I said. "I bet she'd help."

"Mom, can I go to Parker's?" Troy asked. "As you can see, he really needs my detective skills."

"Do you have homework?" she asked.

"I'll do it tonight," Troy said. "I won't watch any TV until it's done, I promise."

"All right," Mrs. Morris said. "But be home by six for dinner. And if you leave Parker's house, call me first."

"Me too!" Eden said. "I want to go play with the dog, too!"

"Not this time," Troy said. "We have important stuff to do. We have a case to solve!" He pushed his glasses up on his nose.

"We'll go home and make brownies instead," Mrs. Morris said to Eden.

"OK," Eden said, beaming.

When we got home, first I called Dad to tell him what happened. Then I called Kristal.

"I'll be there in five minutes," she said. "Can I bring Skye? I'm supposed to be babysitting her."

"Sure," I said. "Don't forget your camera."

Troy and I threw the tennis ball for Merlin while we waited for Kristal. He found the garden hose and pawed at it, trying to make it spray him. But I knew if I did that he would *shake shake shake* as soon as Kristal got there. He'd get her and her sister all wet. That wouldn't be a great way to start our investigation.

Skye came running up to the gate from the side-walk. "Hi Parker! Hi Troy! Hi Merlin!" she called, jumping up and down.

I unlocked the bike lock to let her and Kristal through.

"We should set up the camera in the kitchen window," Troy said. "I think that's the best vantage point." I was pretty sure he'd gotten "vantage point" from a TV show.

"And then we'll all go out the gate and leave him here," Kristal said. "When he catches up to us, we'll come back and watch the video to see what he did."

"OK, but let's not go far," I said. I was still worried about him running around loose.

Kristal and Troy went inside to set up the camera. I let Skye throw the ball for Merlin. He chased after it and she giggled. Then he grabbed it and started running around the yard.

"Bring it back!" Skye called. "Merlin! Bring it back!"

He dropped the ball. "Woof! Woof!" he barked, bouncing on his front paws. She ran toward him and he picked it up and ran away.

"Merlin!" Skye called, laughing.

Troy and Kristal came outside again. I closed the

kitchen door and locked it from the outside, as if I was really leaving. I went over to the gate with the others.

"'Bye, Merlin," I said. "We'll be back soon. Don't be bad."

He was sitting with the ball at the other end of the yard. He tilted his head to the side. His ears scooted forward.

When I opened the gate, he came galloping over. I blocked his way while Troy, Kristal, and Skye went through. "Nope. Sorry, Merlin," I said. I squeezed through the gate and closed it again. He tried to stick his nose in the little gap at the side. I wound the lock through the links and snapped the padlock in place.

"Arooo arooooo," Merlin whimpered in confusion. He pawed at the gate.

"Oh, poor dog," Skye said. She stuck her fingers through the chain links and scratched his head.

"We have to figure this out for his own good," I said. "Come on."

We all went down to the sidewalk and started to walk away toward school. I looked back a couple of times and saw Merlin watching through the fence. "He doesn't look like he's following us," I said.

"He will once he can't see you anymore," Kristal said confidently.

We turned a corner onto Maple Street. The trees here were leafy and green and hung over the street, whispering in the wind. The sun reflected off the windows of the houses. Everything was quiet.

And then . . . "Woof! Woof!"

Merlin barreled into the back of my legs before I could even turn around. He jumped and leaped all around us. He licked Skye's face and she squealed. He seemed to be saying *You guys, you forgot me! But it's OK, I'm here now! Now we can play!*

"Perfect!" Troy said. "Let's go see what he did!"

We ran back to my house. Merlin raced beside us. His fur flew out like sunrise clouds, golden in the light.

Inside, Kristal hit Stop and Rewind on the video camera. She pulled some wires out of the carrying case and hooked the camera up to the TV. I picked up the remote and turned it on. Merlin jumped up on the couch, shaking out his fur and posing like this was a movie premiere and he was the star. Troy and Skye wriggled in on either side of him.

"Here we go!" Kristal said. She hit Play.

We saw ourselves leave the yard. We saw Merlin

watch us sadly through the fence. He pawed at the gate as we went out of sight. He tried to lift the latch with his nose and push it open. When that didn't work, he started pacing back and forth along the fence, whining softly.

After a moment, he ran away from the fence and back up to it a couple of times. Then he crouched down at the foot of the fence. His rear end waggled around. He stared up at the top of the fence.

"No way," Troy breathed.

Merlin pushed down hard with his back legs. He flew up into the air.

With one giant leap, Merlin was on top of the fence!

He teetered there for a long moment. His back half was still inside. His front paws scrabbled on the other side of the fence. He had this goofy *uh-oh!* look on his face. I thought for a moment that he would overbalance and land back inside.

But he managed to hook his back paws in the chain links. He leaned forward and pushed and wiggled and then finally . . .

He was over the fence! He landed on all four paws. He shook himself off, sniffed around the grass for a minute, and then proudly trotted off down the street in the direction we had gone.

Back in my living room, we all turned to stare at Merlin.

"Woof!" my dog said. Like, *Did you see me? Wasn't I fabulous? No autographs, please!* He wagged his tail and rolled sideways so he was nearly upside down in Skye's lap.

"Wow," Skye said, rubbing his belly. "You should be in the circus, Merlin!"

"We did it," Troy said, pleased. "We figured out how he escapes. Mystery solved!"

The mystery was solved. But it didn't help me very much. Sure, now I knew how he was getting out. But what I really needed to know . . . was how to keep him in.

CHAPTER 13

It wasn't the best day ever. And it got worse when Dad came home with Julianne.

"Julianne's going to make us dinner," Dad said. He stage-whispered behind his hand, "Don't worry, she's not a vegetarian." Julianne laughed. She patted Merlin and he licked her hand.

"I'm a terrible cook, actually," Julianne said. "Nowhere near as good as your sister."

"I'm sure you're still better than we are," Dad said.

"I can make one thing," she said. "It involves chicken and pasta and broccoli."

"We don't have any of that," I said. Dad gave me a look like I was being rude. I didn't think it was rude to tell the truth.

"That's OK," Julianne said, "I brought everything I need. Want to help me chop broccoli, Leonard?"

Dad said sure in this excited way, like he'd been wanting to chop broccoli his whole life. Well, *I* wasn't going to help. I took Merlin out in the yard and threw the tennis ball for him. But it felt strange because I knew Dad and Julianne could see me from the window.

Dinner was even stranger. I wished Camellia was there. Even if she didn't like Julianne, she could still talk to her. Now Julianne and Dad just wanted to talk to me. They kept asking me questions about sixth grade. We'd only had two days of it! I had nothing interesting to tell them. The pasta was pretty good, but I just wanted to get away from the table so badly.

"When does baseball practice start?" Julianne asked.

"Not till the spring," I said. "But Coach Mason is organizing a game after school tomorrow to keep us in shape, he said. You can come if you want," I said hopefully to Dad.

"I'll see if I can," he said.

"Maybe I could go," Julianne said. She actually sounded excited about the idea. How odd would that be, though? Would I have to tell my friends who she was? My dad's "girlfriend"? It sounded too weird.

The phone rang. I practically shot out of my chair to get it. I hoped it would be Camellia, or really anyone to get me away from this conversation. But instead it was Alicia from Bark and Ride Day Care.

"Hi Parker," she said. "I've been feeling so bad about kicking Merlin out of day care."

"It's OK," I said. I didn't know why she felt bad. We were the ones with the crazy dog.

"I was thinking about it," Alicia said, "and there's someone you guys could call. He's a dog walker. I checked with him, and he said he could probably fit Merlin in."

"Really?" I said.

"Sure," Alicia said. "Let me tell your dad the details."

"OK. Thanks," I said. I took the phone to Dad. He got up and went to find paper he could write on.

That left me alone at the dinner table with Julianne. I poked a piece of broccoli around the plate with my fork. I could tell she was trying to think of something to say. She's not like me and Dad. We can sit quietly without talking for hours. But Julianne likes to fill up the silence with yapping. Kind of like that Yorkie at the day care center.

"Merlin is lucky he found such a patient family," she said. I realized Merlin was lying under her chair. That dog really didn't know the difference between good people and unnecessary people.

"Yeah," I said.

Dad came back into the room. "Thanks, Russell," he said into the phone and hung up.

"Who's Russell?" Julianne asked before I could.

"Our new dog walker," Dad said with a smile. "We'll take Merlin over there tomorrow morning. Russell can keep Merlin at his house during the day and walk him for us. Isn't that great, Parker?"

It was great, I guessed. But it made me a little sad. I wished we didn't have to leave Merlin with a stranger all day. I wished I could come home to let Merlin out instead. I was sure that would make both Merlin and me much happier.

After dinner, Dad and Julianne watched a movie on the couch. They said I could watch with them, but I said I had homework to do. Merlin, on the other hand, jumped right up and flopped onto Julianne's lap.

"Traitor," I whispered to him, but he just wagged his tail at me.

So I went and hung out in my room by myself. I missed Camellia. She was good at solving problems. I wished she had solved the Julianne problem before leaving.

The next morning we got up early again. Russell only lived a few blocks away, so we walked Merlin over to his house. Merlin was thrilled to be outside.

He kept tugging on his leash and sticking his head into any bushes we passed. By the time we got there, there were bits of leaves and twigs tangled all through his golden fur.

Russell was not what I expected. I had imagined someone young like Mr. Peary. But Russell was older, maybe my dad's age. He was big, with big muscles, and he was bald except for a huge brown walrus mustache. He looked like he should be riding a motorcycle, not taking care of dogs. He made me nervous. He even made Merlin a little nervous. I could tell because Merlin kind of crouched low to the ground when Russell came out to greet us.

"Hey mate," Russell said to Merlin. He had a kind of Australian accent. "I hear you're a regular Houdini!"

"That he is," Dad said, shaking Russell's hand.

"Well, lemme show you what I've got," Russell said. He jerked his thumb at the backyard. "I've never met the dog that can get out of this thing!"

We followed him around to the back of the house. There was no fence around his yard. But there was a fenced-off area of grass in the back. It was about the size of my bedroom. Inside was a bowl of water and a wooden doghouse. One side was the wall at the back of the house. The other three sides were the tallest fence I'd ever seen. It was at least three times as tall as our fence. There was no way Merlin could leap to the top of it. And the gate closed with a padlock.

Russell picked up a Frisbee and threw it to the back of his yard. Merlin bounded to his feet and sped after it. It hit the ground rolling, and Merlin was able to get his jaws around it. He picked it up and came trotting back, swishing his tail back and forth.

"So what I'll do," Russell said, "is keep him with me indoors during the morning. I'll take him out for a break at lunchtime. Then I'll put him in here while I do my afternoon rounds. And I'll bring him back to your place at four thirty, once you're done with school and your baseball game. That sound good to you guys?"

"Sounds great," Dad said. "We appreciate it."

"No worries," Russell said, winking at me.

I made it to school on time again. But I was pretty tired. It was hard to concentrate on Mr. Peary or South American capitals. I kept thinking about Merlin and that big cage. I thought about him inside Russell's house. I bet he was sitting by the window. I bet he was waiting for me to come get him. I hoped he didn't think I had abandoned him. I wasn't like his last two owners. I would never get rid of him like that, no matter how bad or embarrassing he was sometimes.

Danny kicked me and I jumped. Mr. Peary had asked me a question.

"Um," I said. "Buenos Aires?"

Everybody laughed, including Kristal and Natasha and even Eric. Mr. Peary raised his eyebrows at me.

"I don't think the Iroquois ever got to Argentina," he said, "but it's nice to know you were paying attention half an hour ago."

I looked down, embarrassed. Luckily, right then the bell rang for lunch.

"Parker," Mr. Peary said as we all got up to go to the cafeteria, "please see me after school for a few minutes."

"Yes, sir," I said, hoping that wouldn't make me late for the baseball game.

I caught up to Danny and Eric at the cafeteria doors. We got into the line for the school lunch.

"Are you in trouble?" Eric asked.

"Just a little, I think," I said. "Not as much as I was on Monday!"

"You were totally spacing out," Danny joked.

"I just wish I could see Merlin during the day," I said, taking a tray.

"Awwwwwwwwwww," Avery said from right behind me. "Parker misses his wittle puppy."

I rolled my eyes at Danny and Eric but I didn't turn around. I could ignore Avery.

"Whatsa matter?" Avery said. "No girls here to defend you?"

"He's with a dog walker today," I said to Danny, pretending Avery wasn't there. "This guy Russell. Isn't that a cool job? I wouldn't mind being a dog walker."

"That would be awesome!" Danny agreed. We all took plates of meat loaf from the cafeteria guy. "Just hanging out with dogs all day!"

"You might as well," Avery sneered, "since you already smell like one."

I couldn't tell if Avery was talking to me or Danny, but from the look on Danny's face, I guessed it was him.

"You'll smell like a dog when I plant your face in the ground!" Danny said to Avery, leaning around me with his fist up.

"Yeah, right! Just try!" Avery said.

"Hey," I said, pushing Danny back. "Ignore him. He's just being an idiot."

"You think you can scare me off?" Avery snapped at both of us.

"If not, I guess we can always get Heidi to do it, huh?" I said. That made him look really mad. I wondered if he would actually hit me right here in the cafeteria.

Suddenly I heard a girl's voice yell, "Hey, there's a dog! There's a dog coming this way!"

My heart plummeted. Surely it couldn't be . . . ?

Merlin came galloping through the open cafeteria doors. His leash was trailing behind him. He was panting like he'd been running full out. He looked around wildly.

"Dog!" several other kids yelled. A few people jumped on their chairs, pointing.

Finally Merlin spotted me. He raced toward me, his paws skidding on the smooth floor.

"WHERE IS HE?" I heard Vice Principal Taney bellow from outside. "WHERE IS THAT DOG?"

CHAPTER 14

"**U**h-oh," Eric said.

"Think fast!" said Danny. He picked up his meat loaf. And then he threw it right in Avery's face.

"Wh-what?" Avery sputtered. He grabbed his milk and dumped it over Danny's head.

"FOOD FIGHT!" Troy yelled from across the cafeteria.

There was instant pandemonium. I don't know why that happens, but it works every time. And it never matters how much trouble we get in afterward.

Almost all the boys in the room jumped up on their chairs and started hurling food. Tara and Natasha screamed really loud and crawled under their table. I saw Ella leap up and dart out the back exit before she could get hit in the crossfire. That's the difference between those girls — Ella is smart enough to just get out of the way, while Tara and Natasha seem to really like sticking around and screaming and making a fuss instead. Then they spend the rest of the day complaining about how their hair smells like ketchup.

And then there are girls like Heidi, who like throwing food just as much as the guys do. She dumped her tray out on the table and used it as a shield. From behind it, she broke her meat loaf into chunks. That gave her a lot more ammunition than people who threw their entire slice at once. I don't know if she knew that this food fight was to save my dog, but I bet she would love that.

Hugo from the baseball team loves food fights more than anyone. He's very enthusiastic, but not the best strategist. I'm not sure you'd want him on your side in a war, is what I'm saying. This time I saw him fling his entire tray in the air. Left with nothing to throw, he grabbed the nearest kid's meat loaf and threw that.

"Hey!" Pradesh yelled. "That was mine!" He scooped up a giant spoonful of mashed potatoes and flicked it, *SPLAT!* into Hugo's hair.

Even the little kids were getting into it. Most of the first and second graders were shrieking as loudly as Tara and Natasha while they threw their food. Troy's little sister, Eden, had peanut butter and jelly in her hair and an enormous smile on her face.

By the time Vice Principal Taney got to the cafeteria door, the big room was in total chaos.

I grabbed Merlin's leash and ducked below the level of the tables. Merlin covered my face with vigorous licks. He pressed himself close to my side as we ran down one of the aisles between the tables. I didn't dare look over at Vice Principal Taney. I was sure that if I did, he would spot us instantly.

I ran for the door Ella had gone through. We weren't supposed to use it during the day, but it was the fastest route to the music room and the playground. Kids who finished lunch early used it all the time and never got in trouble.

There was a patch of open space between the last table and the door. I glanced around quickly. My heart was pounding.

Vice Principal Taney was waving his arms and shouting angrily. A piece of bologna flew through the air and whapped him on the side of the head. Furious, he turned to see who threw it. His back was to us.

Merlin and I bolted for the door. We shot through it and ran down the hall as the door slowly closed behind us. The hall was empty; most everyone was in the cafeteria. But then . . . were those footsteps? Heels in the hallway? Was it the principal?

I didn't even look back. I threw myself and Merlin into the nearest classroom. We dove behind the teacher's desk — except it wasn't a desk, it was a piano.

We were in the music room!

There was a long moment of tense silence. I leaned against the back of the piano, gasping for breath. Merlin was panting, but his tail was wagging, and he kept sticking his nose in my face, trying to lick me. I tried to scoot him out of sight of the door, but he kept jumping and wriggling. He would be really bad at hide-and-seek.

Suddenly I heard someone moving. I whipped around.

Ella Finegold was sitting on the piano bench. She was leaning way out on the edge so she could see us on the other side of the piano. She blinked at me, looking confused.

"Hi," I said finally.

"Hey Parker," she said. She's so quiet that it always surprises me when she talks and you hear how normal her voice is. I always expect it to be squeakier or more timid or something.

"So," she said. "I'm guessing you're not here to practice for the talent show."

I smiled. "Just catching our breath," I said.

"That's your new dog?"

"Yeah," I said. "Merlin. The biggest troublemaker in dog history."

Ella snorted. "You should meet mine," she said.

She shoved back her long brown curls like they were getting in her way.

"You have a dog?" I was astonished. "But — I thought you didn't like dogs."

"I don't really," Ella said. "Especially this one. We inherited her a few days ago. She's a royal pain." She shrugged.

Merlin bumped my chin with his head. He sat down and leaned into me, wagging his tail. I put my arm around him. "They're worth it, though," I said. "I think. I hope. Eventually." If only Merlin would stop getting me in so much trouble!

"I doubt it," Ella said. "I mean, mine, anyway. This is the only place I can get any peace and quiet from her." She touched the music in front of her. My dad signed me up for guitar lessons one summer, but I was pretty terrible. I never wanted to practice. I think it's pretty amazing how Ella wants to practice, like, all the time. I guess that's why she'll be famous one day instead of any of the rest of us.

"Sorry to bother you," I said with a twinge of guilt. Merlin and I were causing problems everywhere.

"That's OK," she said. "You want me to check if the hall is empty?"

"Would you?" I said. "Really?"

"Sure," she said. "Stay there."

She went to the doorway and poked her head out. I could see her fingers tapping on the door like she was playing the piano inside her head. I don't think she even knows that she does that. After a moment, she moved a little farther into the hall.

"Hi Mr. Taney," she said loudly. "Why are you tiptoeing down the hall?"

"Hssssst." I heard Mr. Taney shushing her. "Have you seen a dog come this way, Miss Finegold?"

"A dog?" Ella said. "Do you mean a hot dog? I think it was meat loaf day today, sir, not hot dogs."

"No, no!" Mr. Taney snapped. "An actual dog! Fur! Paws! Drool! Sanitation hazard!"

"A *real* dog!" Ella exclaimed. "What kind of dog?"

"Any kind of dog!" Mr. Taney shouted, exasperated. "If you've seen *any dog* running down this hallway, I want to know about it!"

"Gee, I'm sorry, Mr. Taney," Ella said, sounding hurt. "I haven't seen any dogs running down this hallway. I didn't mean to make you *shout* at me." She sniffled a little. I couldn't see her face, but she sounded like he'd really upset her. It was an ace performance.

"They must have gone the other way," the vice principal muttered. "I'll go around and cut them off!" I heard his footsteps running away down the hall.

"All right, coast is clear," Ella said, coming back into the music room.

"That was awesome!" I said, climbing to my feet. Merlin jumped to his paws beside me. "You saved our butts. You should be an actress! You're totally hilarious."

She blushed. "Oh, no, I just like to sing," she said.

"Well, thanks," I said. "See you later."

I peeked into the hall again. As Ella had said, the coast was clear. Wrapping Merlin's leash firmly around my hand, I tugged him behind me out of the room. We ran down the hall toward the playground, in the opposite direction from Mr. Taney.

I didn't know what to do. Should I try running home and leaving Merlin there? Was there enough time before the end of lunch? Would I get in trouble for leaving school without permission? I didn't think the principal would be so nice about strike two. Especially after that food fight. Vice Principal Taney was probably really mad right now.

I felt around in my pockets. I didn't want to bother Dad at work again if I could come up with something else. Did I have Russell's phone number? Maybe I could call him to come get Merlin. I wondered how Merlin had gotten away. Since he had his leash on, maybe it was during one of his walks.

There was a card in my jacket pocket. I pulled it out and realized it was the one with Julianne's number on it. No. No way. I was not calling her.

I got to the playground door and looked out. A black iron fence stood between the playground and the quiet street outside. Once I was through that gate, we'd only be a few blocks from home. I figured I had to risk it. Maybe with the chaos of the food fight, no one would notice I was gone.

But then I saw someone running along the sidewalk.

It was Russell!

I burst through the door and ran across the playground with Merlin galloping beside me. Russell was gasping and breathing heavily. He was trying to run, but he was a pretty big guy, and not that young. He was kind of floundering along. His face was bright red behind the walrus mustache.

When he saw me and Merlin, he nearly collapsed to the sidewalk. His face was so relieved, I couldn't be mad at him for losing Merlin. Especially when I knew it was most likely Merlin's fault.

"Oh, man," he said. "Parker, I am real sorry,

mate. I can't even — you have no — I was so —" He stopped, wheezing for breath. I was afraid he would keel over right there. Instead he knelt down and put his arms around Merlin. "Thank the saints you're all right, dog. One moment I was holding him, and he was trotting along just fine, and then all of a sudden he bolted. The leash slipped out of my hands. I've never had that happen to me before, and I've been walking dogs for years."

Merlin licked Russell's face like he was maybe a little bit sorry for making Russell run and worry so much.

"It's OK," I said, "but please, you have to get him out of here right now. My vice principal is on the warpath, and if he catches me out here with Merlin, I'll be in *huge* trouble."

"No worries," Russell said, leaping to his feet with renewed energy. "We were never here! You never saw us!" He wrapped Merlin's leash firmly around his fist and set off at a brisk trot. Merlin looked back at me and whined, trying to pull away, but Russell was too strong. Soon they were jogging around the corner and out of sight.

I let out a breath I didn't know I'd been holding. I glanced at my watch. Almost the end of the lunch hour. I ran back across the playground into the school.

Could I make it into the cafeteria without being spotted by Mr. Taney? I doubted it.

Then I heard the squeak of Mr. Taney's shoes coming down the next hallway. There was only one place to go. I darted into Mr. Peary's classroom and flew across the room into my seat. Luckily Mr. Peary wasn't at his desk. The room was empty.

I dug through my bag and pulled out a notebook as fast as possible.

The door flew open.

Vice Principal Taney stood there, glaring. His face was almost purple with anger. And he had a tiny smear of bright yellow mustard on his left ear. I decided I probably shouldn't tell him about that.

"Mr. Green," he said in his most dangerous, most ominous voice. "What — *what* — pray tell, are you doing in here?"

I glanced around like I couldn't understand the question. "This is my classroom, sir. I thought we were allowed to be in our classrooms during lunch."

He advanced slowly across the room. "Only if you are engaged in academic pursuits."

"I am," I said, "um, engaged in . . . that, sir." I held up the notebook. "I'm studying for our spelling test this afternoon." Miraculously, I had grabbed the right notebook. Even if Mr. Taney checked, he would find out that it was true. We were scheduled to have a spelling test that afternoon.

"That's *unusually industrious* of you," Vice Principal Taney said. He stopped next to my desk and seized the notebook. His eyes scanned the list of words. He looked down at me suspiciously.

"Have you seen your dog today, Mr. Green?"

"Sure," I said. His nostrils flared angrily. "At home this morning, sir," I added quickly. "We dropped him off with a dog walker for the day. Now he has someone to keep an eye on him! It's such a relief. I would be *so* embarrassed if he showed up here again!"

All of this was true. I was trying to keep Camellia's honesty rules in mind. But then again, I think even Camellia wouldn't want me to get expelled because of Merlin. Then it would be her fault if I didn't graduate high school and I ended up living in Dad's basement for the rest of my life.

Mr. Taney narrowed his eyes. He stared at me for a long, awful moment.

Finally he dropped the notebook on my desk and stalked out of the classroom without another word.

I fell back in my seat with a great whoosh of air. That was way, way too close.

CHAPTER 15

Principal Hansberry came to each of our classrooms that afternoon to talk to us about discipline and wasting food and respecting the cafeteria workers. I was really worried that Danny would be suspended for starting the food fight. He'd only been helping me. If he got in trouble, I'd have to come clean and take his punishment instead.

But the principal had decided that this was "first-week high spirits." Instead of singling out anyone for punishment, she made the whole school use the last hour of the day to help clean up the cafeteria. That was the first time we'd been punished like that for a food fight. We all got to see what a huge gross mess we had left behind. Lots of kids complained that they hadn't thrown any food, but Principal Hansberry said that since making the mess was a "group effort," cleaning it up should be, too.

Plus we all had to write a note to take home that said, "Dear Mom and Dad, I am sorry if I have ketchup or anything on my clothes today. We were involved in a food fight at lunch, and we feel very bad for causing so much trouble. Please accept my apology for the extra laundry." Personally, I thought this was kind of a funny note. But we had to bring it back signed by our parents, so a lot of people didn't think it was so funny.

Luckily they weren't mad at me or Danny, though. Except for Avery. He tried to get Danny in trouble by telling Principal Hansberry who'd started the fight. But she told him that wasn't necessary. She said everyone was "responsible for the mob mentality we saw here today," whatever that means.

The most amazing part was that nobody said anything about Merlin. I guess a lot of people didn't see him. But even the ones who did didn't admit it. Vice Principal Taney came into our class and asked: "Did anyone here see a dog in the cafeteria before or during the food fight?"

No one raised their hands. After a minute, Heidi said: "Maybe you imagined it, Mr. Taney," in this really innocent voice.

I was worried that Avery would tell, but later Hugo told me that nobody in Mr. Guare's class answered Mr. Taney's question either. I don't know why Avery didn't say anything. Maybe he already knew everyone was mad at him for snitching on Danny.

Cleaning up the cafeteria was gross, but it wasn't too terrible. I felt really guilty and grateful to everyone for not telling, so I worked as hard as I could. I mopped and I wiped down the tables and I helped clean the windows and I filled an entire trash bag with squashed meat loaf. I was used to cleaning — that's something Camellia trained me to do really early. She always said if she had to cook, then Dad and I had to learn how to clean.

At the end of the hour, Mr. Peary came up to me where I was wiping down the door handles. He said, "Nice work, Parker. You represented our class very well. I'll let you off for not paying attention in class earlier today — but try not to let it happen again."

"Yes, Mr. Peary," I said.

The best thing about our punishment was that it ended when school was over. Which meant it didn't get in the way of the baseball game. I was pretty excited. Danny and Eric and Troy and I had practiced together all summer in the park. I was hoping the coach would notice how much better I'd gotten.

"Come on, come on!" Danny said, shaking my

arm as I dumped my last handful of dirty paper towels in the garbage. "Let's get out to the field! Coach Mason will be waiting!"

We grabbed our stuff from the classroom and ran out to the baseball field behind the gym. Most of the guys were already there, including Troy and Hugo and Levi, from our class. Coach Mason was walking around the bases, tossing a ball into the mitt on his left hand. He was wearing the Red Sox cap he always wears. He says, "You can take the man out of Boston, but you can't take Fenway out of the man."

He's also the coach for the girls' team, so a lot of them had come to watch. Heidi and Rory waved to us from the bleachers. Coach Mason is Rory's dad. She's crazy-athletic like Danny is. Troy's mom was there, too, and so was Danny's dad — he never misses a baseball game, even when it's just for fun like this one.

My dad wasn't there, but that was OK. I know it's hard for him to get away from the bank during the day. But then, scanning the bleachers, I saw a familiar face.

Julianne was there! I couldn't believe it. I didn't think she meant it when she said she wanted to come.

"Oh, man," I muttered.

"What?" Danny asked.

I was going to pretend it was nothing. Part of me didn't want to tell Danny that my dad had a girlfriend. Especially one who was only about ten years older than Camellia. But Julianne was already waving and smiling at me. Danny saw her and his eyebrows went up.

"Who's that?" he asked. "Do you *know* her? Is that her real hair color?"

"That's my dad's new girlfriend," I said with a sigh.

"Wow," Danny said. "Go Mr. Green!"

"Shut up. Gross!" I said, punching him on the shoulder.

I tried not to look over at her while Coach divided us into teams. Troy and Eric and I were on one team and Danny was on the other. This was bad news. Danny is pretty good at baseball. But it's not only that. He plays like a crazy person. If he's running to a base, and you're standing on it waiting to catch a ball, he will throw himself into a full-on dive straight at your feet. He knocks people over when he's tagging them out all the time. He just gets really excited, like Hugo in a food fight, or Merlin pretty much anytime.

We flipped a coin, and my team was up to bat

first. Danny went "WOO! WOOOOO!" and ran out to second base, pumping his arms in the air. Heidi yelled "WOOOOOO!" back at him and he grinned, jumping up and down.

I kicked the dirt around the bench, keeping my head down so I wouldn't accidentally meet Julianne's eyes. But when I heard Troy's bat connect with the ball, I jumped to my feet with the rest of the team.

"Run!" I yelled. "Ruuuuuun!" Troy was sprinting to first base. Levi was waiting there with his mitt raised. The ball flew through the air — and right past his hand. Troy sprinted to first. Everybody cheered. I couldn't help glancing at Julianne. But she wasn't watching me. She had her eyes glued on the game.

Eric was up next. He gripped the bat tightly in his hands. Troy pushed his glasses up and inched toward second. He leaned forward, waiting. We all leaned forward.

Hugo pitched the ball. *Crack!* Eric slugged it! The baseball shot into the air. It went way over Danny's head. It zoomed into the outfield. Danny and three other guys ran after it. Troy dashed to second and then kept going to third. Right behind him, Eric touched first base and kept running. He landed on second, took another step, and then jumped back onto the base. Danny was too close. He came running up with the ball and stood looking at Eric like, *Don't you want to try running?* Eric grinned at him. Danny threw the ball back to the pitcher.

Now it was my turn. The bat was smooth under my palms. I swung it around a little, knocking it against my shoes. I got into batting position. I didn't look at the bleachers. I was afraid Julianne would yell my name. That would be even more embarrassing than chasing Merlin around the playground. But she didn't say anything.

Whoosh!

"Ball one!" Coach Mason called.

"What?" Hugo yelled. "That was totally a strike!"

"Hugo," Coach said warningly. Hugo just likes arguing. He watches the games on TV hoping there will be a ruckus on the field. He loves yelling at the umpires for no reason. He doesn't pay that much attention to the actual rules.

The catcher threw it back. Hugo wound up.

Whoosh!

"Strike one!" Coach called.

I wanted to do this right. Two players were on base. It would be so awesome if I scored two runs in my first hit of the year. Maybe even a home run as well! I crouched, giving Hugo the eagle eye. Here it came. . . .

Thwack!

The ball soared into the air. It didn't go as high as Eric's, but it went farther. It hit the ground and rolled between two of the outfielders. I was already running to first base.

Out of the corner of my eye, I saw a blur of something moving.

Something that was not a baseball player.

Something golden . . . and furry.

"HEY!" one of the outfielders yelled. "That dog took the baseball!"

Please no, I prayed. I hit first base and kept running. But as I rounded the corner toward second, I saw Merlin. He was galloping triumphantly toward me with the ball in his mouth. The outfielders were chasing him, waving their arms. Merlin looked absolutely delighted with himself.

"Merlin!" I shouted. I stopped dead. Merlin ran up to me, bounded in a circle around me, and bopped me with his nose. I reached for the ball and he dashed away.

Troy had made it to home base, but Eric was standing between third base and home, looking confused. "Does that count?" he called. "Are we still playing?"

"Merlin tagged him out!" Danny shouted. "You saw it! He tagged Parker out!" He ran after Merlin. People in the stands were laughing so hard, they were practically falling off the bleachers.

"Booooo!" Rory yelled. "Too many players on the field! Foul!"

"Yeah, go Merlin!" Heidi shouted. "MVP! Give that dog a trophy!"

"What's going on?" Coach Mason bellowed. "Who is that dog?"

I decided that running after Merlin would be easier than explaining things to Coach Mason. Danny and I chased my dog around and around the field. This, unfortunately, was pretty much Merlin's dream come true. His paws flew over the dirt. He stopped, waited for us to nearly catch up, and then dodged around us to run away again.

Soon all the guys on the team were chasing him. He wasn't wearing his leash this time, so it was even harder to catch him. How had he gotten away from Russell *twice*? I couldn't understand it.

Finally we cornered Merlin by the fence. I lunged forward and grabbed his collar. He dropped the ball right away. The guys all applauded.

"*Merlin*," I said. "I can't even *believe* how bad you are!"

He wagged his tail at me.

"Ew, gross," Levi said, picking up the baseball gingerly with two fingers. "It's all slobbery."

"Sorry, guys," I said. "Thanks for helping me catch him."

Coach Mason blew his whistle. We all went back across the field to where he was standing on second base with his hands on his hips. I kept my hand firmly locked around Merlin's collar, although he didn't seem interested in running away anymore. He was just happy to be with me again.

"Green," Coach said. "Is this your dog?"

"I'm really sorry, Coach," I said. "I don't know how he got loose." I looked around for Russell, but there was no sign of him. Maybe he was still trying to catch up. The only good news was that Vice Principal Taney was nowhere to be seen. He didn't usually stick around for sports stuff.

"Well, you'd better take him home, I guess," Coach said.

I nodded sadly. I really wanted to stay for the rest of the game. I wanted to show Coach I'd been practicing. I wanted to show him how good my pitching had gotten. But Merlin was my responsibility. I had to take care of him, and that meant taking him home and missing the game.

"Hey," said a voice behind me.

I turned around. Julianne was at the fence in front of the bleachers, leaning her elbows on the top of it. "I could take him back to your house," she said. "So you can stay for the game."

"Woof!" Merlin barked, like he was agreeing with her.

I was torn. I wanted to stay. But I didn't want Julianne's help. I didn't want her to be in my house by herself. I didn't want her hanging out with Merlin without me. Mostly, I didn't want her to think she was part of our family.

"That's OK, I can do it," I said.

"What?" Troy said, elbowing me. "The team needs you, Parker! Just say yes!"

"Yeah, come on," Danny agreed.

"It's no problem," Julianne said. She held out her hand to Merlin and he leaned toward her, wagging his tail.

"Make up your mind, Green," Coach said. "Everyone else, back to the game." The guys started jogging back to their bases.

All right. Just this once. "OK," I said to Julianne. "Thanks." I led Merlin around the fence to her and she took his collar, scratching behind his ears. I dug in my pocket and gave her my house key.

"We'll be there when you get back," she said. "I'll let your dad know."

They headed off across the field. And Merlin didn't even look upset to be leaving. He trotted beside her, wagging his tail as if this was all perfectly fine with him.

Traitor.

CHAPTER 16

We ended up winning the game. I didn't get the home run I'd been hoping for, but I did make it to home plate twice.

"Good work, team!" Coach Mason called as we headed out. Rory was already chattering away to him as they put away the equipment. I could see her pointing to the bases and making suggestions.

"So how'd he do it?" Troy asked as we walked to the parking lot with his mom and Eden. I could tell he'd been waiting the whole game to ask me this. "Didn't you say Russell has a huge fence? How'd Merlin get out?"

"I don't know," I said, shaking my head.

"Your dog is so cool!" Eden said. "And so pretty! And so smart! I wish we had a dog who played baseball!"

"Me too!" Danny chimed in. "I totally want a dog who'll play ball with me."

"I wish he knew *when* to play, though," I said. "And when to stay home!"

Troy wanted to do more investigating, but his mom said it was too close to dinnertime. I made Danny and Eric come home with me, though, so I wouldn't have to talk to Julianne by myself.

When we got there, we found Julianne throwing a Frisbee for Merlin in the backyard. He came running up to the gate when he saw us. I started to unlock the bike lock, and then he jumped right over the fence. He didn't even pretend like he didn't know how. He jumped up on me and then he jumped on Danny and then he ran in circles around Eric.

"Hey guys," Julianne said. "Thank goodness you're here. My arm is so tired." She sat down on the back steps, rubbing her right shoulder. "This dog has ridiculous energy!"

"Yeah," I said, closing the gate behind us as we all went through into the yard.

"He's like Danny that way!" Eric joked.

Danny laughed. He grabbed the Frisbee and ran to the other end of the yard with Merlin chasing him.

"Did Russell call?" I asked.

"I called him," she said. "He had just found out Merlin was gone. He was really freaking out."

"Poor guy," I said.

"What happened?" Eric asked.

"He doesn't know. Merlin was in the fenced-in area," Julianne said. "Russell kept saying, 'It's impossible! I don't get it! It's ruddy impossible!'" Her imitation of Russell's Australian accent was pretty funny. Eric laughed, but I managed not to.

"He said if you want to take Merlin over there later, you could try again and see what happens," Julianne said.

"Let's do it!" Eric said. He checked his watch. "Let's go now. I can call my mom. I want to see him escape."

"Me too!" said Danny, running up to us.

"Woof!" Merlin agreed.

"You want to show off, huh?" I asked Merlin, rubbing his head. "OK."

"I'll wait here and tell your dad where you went," Julianne said as I clipped Merlin's leash onto his collar.

We were about a block away from my house when Eric said, "Shouldn't you have said thank you to your dad's girlfriend?"

"Yeah, or introduced us?" Danny asked.

I shrugged. "Whatever. I mean, it's not even that serious. She'll probably be dating someone else by next month."

Danny and Eric exchanged glances, but they were smart enough not to keep talking about it. "Should we call Kristal?" Eric asked, changing the subject. "Try the video-camera trick again?"

"Let's wait until we get there," I suggested. "Maybe we won't need it." I felt like Kristal had already seen enough of Merlin's craziness.

Russell was waiting outside for us. He apologized over and over. He kept rubbing his bald head and mumbling to himself. He looked at Merlin like my dog was the Loch Ness Monster.

We went around to the back. Danny and Eric both went "Oooooooooooooooh" when they saw the height of the fence. Merlin took one look at it and tried to bolt in the other direction. But I had a firm grip on his leash. He scrabbled in the grass, trying to run away. We had to wrestle him into the cage. I unclipped his leash and jumped out through the gate. Russell closed it and padlocked it. Merlin got up on his hind paws, hooked his front paws on the fence links, and went, "aroooo AROOOO."

"We're just trying to figure you out, goofy dog," I said to him, stroking his nose through the chain links. "So do your trick again, OK?"

"Is there somewhere we can watch him from?" Danny asked Russell.

"Yeah, sure," Russell said. "Come on inside." We went into the house and followed Russell up to the second floor. One of the rooms facing the backyard had almost nothing in it except for some sports equipment and a pile of books. There was a big window overlooking the yard. All four of us crowded around it.

Merlin was pacing around the fenced-in area. He stuck his nose inside the doghouse. He pawed at the grass, kicking up clumps of dirt. He poked the gate with his nose.

For a moment he stood there as if he was thinking. He even glanced over his shoulder, like he was making sure that no one was watching him. Then he sidled over to one of the corners and looked around again. Satisfied that no one could see him, he began leaping in the air.

Leap! His nose reached three-quarters of the way up the fence.

Leap! His paws flailed in the air.

Leap! His ears flapped and flapped.

And then suddenly . . . *leap!* His front paws hooked on the chain links. His back paws scrabbled for a hold. He hung for a second, panting.

Merlin was halfway up the fence. He had his left paws hooked in the fence that went one way from the corner, and his right paws hooked in the fence that went the other way. He was braced in the corner.

Now he began to wriggle. Like a real rock climber, he clung on with three paws while he searched for a new paw hold with the fourth. He moved his front left paw up an inch. His back right paw moved up an inch. His toes and claws poked through the chain links. His tail thrashed, keeping him balanced. He reached as far up as he could with his neck, straining to get to the top. Slowly, inch by inch, he pushed himself up.

"No. Way," Eric breathed.

Russell's mouth was hanging open. I'd seen enough.

I ran out of the room and down the stairs. By the time I burst into the backyard, Merlin had reached the very top of the fence. He was teetering on the rail at the top. His back half was still inside. His front paws were sliding down the outside of the fence.

"Merlin!" I shouted.

He froze with the guiltiest expression I've ever seen on a dog. It was like he wanted to say *What? I'm not doing anything!*, but he knew he was busted.

With a final giant effort, he hurled himself forward and leaped to the grass around the fence. Then he slunk over to me. His ears and his tail were hanging down. He knew he was in trouble this time. A few feet away from me, he dropped to his belly and crawled forward, gazing up at me with his big brown eyes. *I'm sorry*, he seemed to be saying. *How was I supposed to know you didn't* want *me to do that?*

I crossed my arms. "You *are* in big trouble," I said to him. "You *should* feel guilty."

Eric and Danny caught up to me. "Troy will be sorry he missed that," Eric said.

"I know it was bad of him," Danny said, "but you have to admit that was impressive."

I sighed. That kind of "impressive" was going to get me expelled.

CHAPTER 17

Merlin completely forgot he was in trouble by the time we got home. He jumped all over Dad and Julianne with his tail going *swish swish swish* all over the place. Apparently Julianne was staying for dinner again. I probably should have expected that. We ordered from my favorite Chinese place, which made me feel a little better, but not much.

"I think Russell has given up on us, too," I said to Dad. "He said he'd call you later."

"Well, don't worry about tomorrow," Dad said. "Julianne says she can come spend the day with Merlin."

I didn't like that. I didn't like it one bit. It wasn't fair that someone I didn't like would get to spend the whole day with Merlin while I was cooped up in school. And then would she stay for dinner *again*? It was like she had practically moved in as soon as Camellia left. What made her think she was part of our family?

Julianne and Dad chatted on and on all the way through dinner. Julianne told him all about my baseball game — at least, the part of it she saw. Dad tried to get me to tell him the rest, but I didn't feel much like talking. There had to be another solution. I had to think of one. I pushed my General Tso's chicken around until I could politely excuse myself. Then Merlin and I ran upstairs and I borrowed the portable phone from Camellia's room.

Camellia answered on the third ring. It sounded like there was a lot of noise in the background. Like there was a party going on in her room. On a Wednesday night?

"Camellia?" I said, sitting down on the floor. I leaned back against my bed, and Merlin flopped into my lap.

"Parker?" She covered the phone and yelled, "Hey, guys, keep it down!" It didn't sound like it got any quieter to me, but she came back on the line. "Hey Parker! What's up? I miss you guys!"

"Yeah, right," I said. Someone screamed, "Hi Parker!" in the background.

"Paloma says hi," Camellia said.

"Who's Paloma?" I asked. "And what kind of name is that?"

"It's about as bad as Camellia, isn't it?" my sister joked. "What's going on there? How's Merlin?"

"He's the best and worst dog ever," I said, scratching behind his ears. I told Camellia all about Bark and Ride Day Care and Alicia and Russell and Vice Principal Taney and the baseball game. And I told her about Julianne.

"I don't know what to do," I finished. "So I've decided you have to come home." I was only half kidding, but she laughed.

"Sorry, Parker," she said. "I can try to think of something, though. At least you don't have to worry about tomorrow."

"Weren't you listening?" I said. "That's the whole point. If I let Julianne help, it's like letting her be part of the family, when we just want her to go away. But if I don't, Merlin's going to keep being a problem."

"Parker!" Camellia said. "Why would you be trying to get rid of Julianne? Dad likes her!"

I was surprised. "But we don't," I said. "I mean, you and me. You don't like her, do you?"

"Well, she's pretty different from us," Camellia said. "But she could be a lot worse. And I think she makes Dad happy."

"But Dad is happy with us," I said.

"And what's he supposed to do when *you* go off to college in seven years?" Camellia asked. "If you think the house is empty now, just imagine what it'll be like then."

Seven years sounded like a ridiculously long time. Why couldn't he get a girlfriend later, then? Like, right before I graduated? Then maybe I'd be OK with it. But I remembered sitting on the couch by myself while Camellia and Dad were at the airport. I pictured Dad here all alone, and I felt sad for him. Isn't that dumb, seven years before it would happen?

"It's probably not even going to work," I said. "I mean, if Russell couldn't manage him, I'm sure Julianne won't be able to. Merlin will escape the minute she turns her back. I bet you anything he shows up at school again."

"I hope not," Camellia said, but she sounded distracted. I could hear someone shouting her name in the background. "Hey, Parker, I'm sorry, I have to go. But I'll let you know if I have any great ideas, OK?"

"OK," I said.

I didn't feel any better. I tried to do my homework, but I kept spacing out and staring at the page. I thought about Merlin scaling crazy-high fences to get to me. He really didn't mean to be bad. He was happy right now, just lying on my feet.

"Is it because you're worried?" I said to him. "Do you think I might leave you and not come back? I'm not like that, Merlin. I'm not like your other owners. I'll always come back." His tail thumped on the floor. Poor dog. I wished I had a way to make him understand.

The next morning I left early, before Julianne got there. What Camellia had said made sense, but I still didn't want to hang out with Julianne if I could avoid it. And I was sure I'd have to see her again that night anyway.

I looked back at the end of the block and saw Merlin standing up on our couch, watching me out the window. He looked confused and forlorn. I hoped he didn't have some Houdini way of getting through windows, too. If only it were the end of the day already.

When I got to school, about fifteen minutes before the first bell, I saw a couple of kids from my grade outside. Tara and Natasha were sitting on one of the benches, sharing a Pop-Tart. Avery was kicking a rock around the playground. None of them were exactly my favorite people to hang out with. I kept my head down and went to sit on the steps. I pulled out my homework and tried to finish the math problem that I couldn't concentrate on the night before.

I heard giggling and whispering, but I tried to ignore it. Tara and Natasha could have been talking about anything.

"Hi Parker!"

I looked up. The two girls had come over to me. Tara sat on the steps on one side of me, one step up, and Natasha perched on the rail on the other side.

"So where's your dog?" Tara asked. She wound one of her thin little braids around her finger. Natasha giggled.

"Yeah, Parker, where's your dog?" Avery yelled from the other side of the playground.

"Shut up, Avery!" Tara shouted back. "We're trying to have a conversation here!"

Natasha giggled again. She tossed her long dark hair back over her shoulder. Her glasses sparkled a little in the sun. When I looked up at her, she looked away really fast.

"Merlin's at home," I said.

"He's really pretty," Tara said. "Right, Natasha? Isn't he pretty?"

"Yeah, *so* pretty," Natasha said, and giggled again. "Much prettier than your dog, Tara!"

"My dog is crazy," Tara said. "Hey Parker, maybe sometime if you're going to the dog run, you could call us, and we could bring Bananas to play with

Merlin." She gave Natasha this weird look with her eyes bugging out. I had no idea what that meant. I did think it was funny that she'd included Natasha in the invitation, even though it was Tara's dog.

"Maybe sometime," I said, although I could not imagine myself ever, ever picking up a phone to call either one of them.

"That'd be cool," Tara said. "Wouldn't that be cool, Natasha?"

"Sure," Natasha said, fiddling with her hair. Her face was a little pink, which was strange because it wasn't a very hot day.

"So, Parker, what do you think of Mr. Pear —" Tara started to say, but all of a sudden . . .

BWAAAAAAAAAAAAAAAAAAAAAAAAAAP!!!

Tara shrieked and leaped off the steps. Natasha yelped, too, and nearly fell off the railing. I'll admit it, even I jumped.

Avery had snuck up behind us. He was holding an air horn, the kind that make the loud noise you hear at baseball games. He'd set it off right behind Tara. Now he was laughing and laughing.

"Oh, *Parker*," he said in a simpering voice. "Your dog is so *pretty*."

"Avery, you are such a jerk!" Tara snapped.

"Takes one to know one," he said.

"Oh, that's clever," she said. "Very witty. Write that down so history can remember it."

Avery scowled and stomped away.

"Gosh, that scared me!" Natasha said. "Didn't it scare you, Parker?"

I nodded, but my mind was somewhere else. It was hard to believe, but Avery Lafitte had just given me the perfect solution.

CHAPTER 18

I couldn't wait for school to be over. That was true most days, but today more than ever, because I wanted to rush home and work on my idea. I didn't even care that Julianne would be there.

I tried really hard to listen to Mr. Peary, but by the end of the day the margins of my notes were full of scribbled ideas. Luckily he didn't call on me and catch me daydreaming this time.

Finally the last bell rang. I nudged Danny and leaned over to include Eric, too. "You guys want to come over and help me with something?" I said.

"Yeah, totally," Danny said.

We found Troy outside, waiting with his little sister. When his mom pulled up, he talked her into letting him come with us. She gave him the same speech about being home for dinner and not leaving my house. As soon as she pulled away with Eden, the four of us started running.

We raced all the way back to my house. Of course

Danny won, but I wasn't very far behind. I could see Merlin watching out the window for us. That gave me an extra burst of speed at the end. When he saw us come around the corner, he started barking and barking. It was funny, because I couldn't hear him through the glass, but I could see his mouth moving and his ears flapping back.

Julianne opened the back door as we came through the gate into the yard. Merlin flew across the grass toward me. He leaped and danced and spun in circles, woofing and pawing at me. Julianne laughed.

"Hey buddy," I said, dropping to my knees and rumpling Merlin's fur. "I know, I missed you, too! Did you have a good day?"

"I hope so," Julianne said as if I'd been talking to her. "We watched a lot of TV, I'm afraid. But we played out here for a while, too. He headed for the fence a couple of times, but I was able to distract him with the tennis ball or the Frisbee, thank goodness. I had visions of chasing him down the street all the way to your school! But you were a good boy, weren't you, Merlin? As long as I played with you, you figured you'd stick around."

I was glad Merlin hadn't showed up at school. But I was also jealous. I didn't want Julianne to be a good enough substitute for me in Merlin's mind. She was already trying to replace Camellia. I wouldn't let her replace me, too.

Eric kicked my ankle surreptitiously. He nodded at Julianne.

"Oh," I said. "Yeah, um, thanks. Thanks for hanging out with him."

"No problem — it was fun," she said with a huge smile.

Then Danny kicked my other ankle and raised his eyebrows.

"By the way," I said, rolling my eyes at him, "this is Danny. And Eric and Troy. Guys, this is Julianne." They all said hi.

She beamed at all of us like I'd just invited her into our secret clubhouse or something. "Nice to meet you guys!" she said. "Lucky Merlin, to have so many friends. Well, I'd better be going."

"Going?" I echoed. I nearly said, "You're not staying for dinner?" but I stopped myself in time. I didn't want to sound like I was inviting her to do that.

"Yeah, I'm trying to clean up my portfolio for this gallery in New York," she said. "Doesn't that sound ridiculous? I feel like such an art snob talking about portfolios and galleries. But it's just this little place. It's a long shot. Anyway, we'll see. So I should go."

"OK, 'bye," I said.

"'Bye," Troy and Eric said at the same time.

"Good luck with your portfolio!" Danny said warmly. She smiled again and I felt a little bad that I hadn't even thought to say something like that. Too bad Danny and I couldn't trade places. He'd probably be much nicer to his dad's girlfriend than I could be.

As soon as she was gone, I explained my idea to the guys and we started searching through the garage. I was sure there was something in here we could use. Merlin stayed close to me, poking his nose into every box. This time I remembered to hide Camellia's stuffed animals from him before he found them.

Troy found the first thing we needed. It was still attached to Camellia's old bike. My dad had bought it for her when she first started riding around the neighborhood by herself. He was really nervous that something might happen to her. It was soon after Mom left, and Dad was dealing with us by himself. He was afraid of cars and everything else on the road.

So he bought her the loudest bike horn in the history of the world.

Troy squeezed the black rubber bulb at one end. The horn went *BWAAAAAAAMP!* Even though we were looking at him when he did it, all of us jumped a mile — including Merlin. Perfect!

Danny helped me move things away from the back wall until we found the pile of scrap wood my dad has been gathering for years and years. He has a new plan for it every summer. Maybe he'll build a deck! Or a treehouse! Or a sawhorse. Sometimes he even buys a book on woodworking and stares at it for a few days before giving up. But he keeps adding to the pile of wood "just in case." Whenever he sees a piece of scrap wood by the side of the road, he brings it home. Camellia loves to tease him about it.

And now we were finally finding a use for it! Well, some of it. Just one piece, actually. One long, narrow piece of wood.

I grabbed the roll of string from the workbench and we dragged the piece of wood out to the fence. Merlin trotted along beside us, sniffing the wood curiously. He tried to get his teeth around it, but we took it away from him.

Inside the yard, he ran in big circles while we stood by the fence, trying to rig up my genius device. It was really lucky there were four of us. Danny and Eric each took one end. They held it up level with the top rail of the fence, only a couple of inches away from it. I stuck the rubber bulb of the bike horn between the wood and the rail. We moved and fiddled and tweaked everything until the wood was just far enough from the rail to hold up the horn without making the noise go off. Then Troy ran along the fence, tying the wood to the fence rail at exactly that distance.

When he was done, we carefully . . . carefully . . . let go.

The long bar of wood stayed in place. The bike horn was trapped between it and the fence rail. And hopefully — if this worked — putting any pressure on the wood would make the horn go off. Like, say, if you hit it with your front paws.

This was only part one of my plan, though. Part two was convincing Merlin that I would come back, every time. I ran inside and got his bag of treats. I locked the door as I came out, as if we were really leaving. Merlin was flabbergasted. He dropped the tennis ball and stared at me in disbelief. *How can you be leaving already?* he seemed to be thinking. *We haven't even played at all!*

At the fence we had to do some crazy maneuvering to get under the board and out through the gate without letting Merlin out. But we managed to make it to the other side with my device still intact. I wrapped the bike chain through the links, but I didn't lock it. I had a feeling Merlin would go for jumping the fence every time now that he thought it was easier than opening the gate.

He trotted back and forth along the fence, watching me.

"'Bye, Merlin!" I said. "We'll be right back!"

Troy ran around the hedge into our neighbor's yard, in case Merlin did get over the fence and made a run for it. Danny climbed his tree again so he could watch what Merlin did. Eric came with me. We waved to Merlin and walked away down the street.

We weren't even halfway down the block when we heard *BWAAAAAAAAAMP!* I turned around, half afraid that Merlin would be running up behind me. But there was no sign of him.

"Let's wait a sec," I said, stopping out of sight of the house.

"This is a pretty cool idea," Eric said. "Houdini would totally have done something like this. I mean, if he had a dog like yours. You know he designed a lot of the trick boxes he worked with?"

"That's cool. I hope this works," I said. We started walking back to the house.

Merlin was sitting on the other side of the fence, looking up at the bike horn. When he saw us he leaped to his paws and barked excitedly. His tail whisked back and forth. He crouched and made a jump for the top of the fence.

His paws hit the wooden board. They pressed it

back toward the fence. The bike horn was squeezed between the wood and the fence rail.

BWAAAAAAAAAAAAMP!

Startled, Merlin lost his momentum and fell back to the ground. He shook himself and looked around with this hilarious bewildered expression. I waited another minute until he was calm again. He sat back down and looked at me, tilting his head.

"Hey buddy," I said, coming up to the gate. I crouched to get to eye level with him. "See? I came back." I fed him a treat through the chain links. "Good boy. Good stay."

"That was the funniest thing I ever saw!" Danny called down from the tree. "The look on his face! When the horn went off the first time — it was like a squirrel had just landed on his head. He had no idea what it was, but it made him get away from the fence really fast. Ha!" Danny started laughing again.

I said good-bye to Merlin again while Troy and Eric traded places. Troy and I headed down the block. Again we heard *BWAAAAAAAAAAAAMP!* behind us.

We stopped and waited. Silence.

"I wish we could get a dog," Troy said wistfully. "Maybe a bloodhound, like the kind that help the police find missing people and solve crimes and stuff."

"Then he could come over and play with Merlin," I said. "That'd be awesome. You know, whenever he's not out solving mysteries."

We headed back and the same thing happened again. When Merlin saw us, he went bonkers. He barked and jumped and spun and then he tried to leap up to jump over the fence. But as soon as his paws hit the board, *BWAAAAAAAAMP!* He fell back, shook himself, and stood there looking startled.

Again I waited until he was calm, and then I went up and fed him another treat. "Good boy," I said. "And here I am again. Just like I promised."

Merlin wagged his tail.

"You guys don't have to stick around for this," I said to my friends. "I bet it's super-boring for you. I just have to keep doing this until he stops trying to get out."

"I want to stay," Troy said.

"Me too," said Eric.

"Me too, as long as we go to the park eventually," Danny said with a grin.

I grinned back. Julianne was right about one thing. Merlin and I were lucky to have friends like these.

CHAPTER 19

Later that night I told Dad about my brilliant plan and how well it had worked. After half an hour, Merlin had stopped trying to jump up on the fence. He waited patiently by the gate until I came back. I stayed away for a little longer each time, but every time I came back and praised him and gave him a treat. And then at the end we took him to the park and let him run around for a while. We even played his favorite game of chasing him while he kept the ball away from us.

"He did so great!" I said, rubbing Merlin's head proudly. "So we'll keep practicing that until he never tries to get out anymore." Merlin looked up at me, panting and grinning. He was tired from all the playing, but he seemed to know he'd been a good dog that day.

We were out on the back steps, watching Dad grill hamburgers for dinner. I forgot there is one thing he knows how to cook. Hamburgers grilling is probably one of my favorite smells. It was still pretty light out, and I could almost pretend it was still summer.

"Nice work, Parker," Dad said. "That's some smart thinking."

"Thanks," I said. I patted Merlin for a minute. I had a question, but I wasn't sure whether to ask it. Finally I just blurted it out. "How come Julianne didn't stay for dinner tonight?"

Dad looked at me sideways. "Did you want her to?"

"Well," I said. "I mean, not always, I just — well, since she stayed with Merlin today — I just thought she would." I shuffled my sneakers in the grass. "You guys aren't breaking up, are you?"

"Gosh, no," Dad said, surprised. I was surprised, too — surprised to find out I was glad about that.

"I thought about asking her to stay," Dad went on, "but I wanted to just hang out with you tonight." He flipped one of the burgers and winked at me. "Besides, there's a baseball game on later. We could watch it if you finish your homework."

"Awesome," I said. I tried to play it cool. I was kind of glad I didn't have a tail like Merlin's, because right then it would probably have been wagging pretty hard.

"Speaking of Julianne," Dad said, "I think we

might have worked out a solution for Merlin, especially now that you've started training him so well." He pointed his spatula at me. "But it comes with some conditions."

"Uh-oh," I said.

"First, Mondays," Dad said. "I've arranged it at work so I have a stretch in the middle of the day with no meetings. I can come home and let him out. I wish I could do that for the other days, but it's too busy."

"I understand," I said. "Merlin will be psyched to see you."

"Tuesdays, Thursdays, and Fridays," Dad continued, "Julianne says she can either stop by or spend the day with Merlin."

"Really?" I said. "All of those days? She doesn't mind?" That wasn't the kind of thing someone did if they were planning on breaking up with your dad. Right?

"She says Merlin is the greatest dog," Dad said. Well, I certainly agreed with that. It was hard not to like someone who felt that way about your dog. "She says he's inspiring, and she could use the exercise."

"That's amazing," I said. Merlin made a quiet snuffling-woofing noise. I realized he'd fallen asleep on my lap and was dreaming. His paws twitched as if he was racing around the park in his dreams. "So that just leaves Wednesdays."

"This is where the conditions come in," Dad said. "I talked to your principal."

"Mrs. Hansberry?" I said.

"Because you have good grades and you've always been a good kid, I was able to talk her into a trial period for this plan. On Wednesdays, you can come home during lunch and let him out yourself."

"What?" I yelped. Merlin shot awake and sat up, blinking. "Are you serious? Dad, are you serious?"

"Quite serious," he said, his eyes twinkling. "But you must get back to school by the end of the lunch hour. You must still eat lunch, although you can eat it here if you want. And you must keep up your grades. If she thinks this is too much of a distraction or too much responsibility, or if I decide it isn't working for you, we'll find something else to do."

I jumped up and pumped my fists in the air.

"Woof!" Merlin agreed happily, bouncing on his paws. "Woof! Woof!"

"I'll do it!" I said. "I swear, my grades will be perfect and I'll be on time all the time. And I'll keep training him so he'll learn not to run away anymore. Merlin, did you hear that?"

"Woof!"

This was more perfect than I could have hoped. Now I'd have something to look forward to in the middle of the school week. Even if it was only on Wednesdays, I'd get to escape and see Merlin during the day. This was the best plan I had ever heard in my entire life.

"Julianne thought you'd be happy about that," Dad said, smiling. "It was her idea. She says that you've been working really hard to take care of Merlin and be responsible for him. It's a lot to ask of an eleven-year-old. I want you to know we're here to help you."

I sat down again and thought about all the people who had helped me with Merlin. Troy and Danny and Eric, of course. And Kristal and Skye. Camellia. Dad and Julianne. Alicia and Russell. Even Ella Finegold. If it hadn't been for her and Danny and Russell on the day of the food fight, Merlin and I would have been totally doomed.

Merlin had to learn to trust that I would always come back for him, so he didn't have to run away to find me. And I had to learn to trust other people to help me take care of him. Even Dad's new girlfriend.

Merlin sat down next to me and we leaned

into each other. He tilted his head back and licked my ear.

"See, Merlin?" I said to him, burying my hands in his golden fur as I hugged him. "I knew it. You're not such a bad dog after all."

Trumpet is a great dog ...
when she isn't getting into trouble!

Pet Trouble
Loudest Beagle on the Block

Turn the page for a sneak peek!

"IT'S ALIIIIIIIIIIIVE!" my brother, Isaac, yelled at the top of his lungs, like a swamp creature had popped out of the ground or something. And by the way, this is not the best thing to yell in a cemetery. I saw people at a funeral halfway up the next hill all turn around to stare at us.

The bag wriggled like crazy in the lawyer's hands. I jumped back. "It *is* alive!" I squeaked.

"What on earth is in there?" Mom demanded. Dad leaned down and peeked inside.

"AROOOOOOOOOOOOOOOOOOOOOOOOO OOOOOOOOOOOO!" went the bag. It was the loudest howl I'd ever heard.

"Oh, wow," Dad said. "Ella, look."

I edged closer and peeked through the mesh. A pair of enormous brown eyes met mine. Two white paws were pressed up to the screen.

"It's a dog!" I gasped.

"Awwrrrooo," the bag said sadly. The dog poked its wet black nose at me and scratched the mesh screen with its claws.

"I didn't know Aunt Golda had a dog," my mom said, looking confused. "Why would she leave it to Ella?"

"She didn't have it very long. I have all its paperwork here," the lawyer said, handing my Dad a manila envelope. Before Dad could say anything else, the lawyer leaped back into his car and drove away.

"AWWWRRROOOOOOOOOO," the dog went again.

"I guess we take it home with us," Dad said.

We all jumped into our car. I dumped the dog carrier on the seat between me and Isaac.

My dad opened the manila envelope. "This says it's a she," he said. "And her name is Trumpet."

I took the zipper at the top of the bag and pulled it slowly. Before I'd gotten it open very far, a shiny black nose appeared in the opening. The dog poked and wriggled like she thought she could fit her whole body out through that tiny hole if she just tried hard enough. I pulled the zipper the rest of the way and the top of the bag peeled back.

An explosion of fur flew out of the bag. Before I could even blink, a white-and-brown blur leaped onto my dress and tried to climb up onto my shoulders. I shrieked as the dog started licking my face with a big, pink, surprisingly scratchy tongue.

"Awww, she likes you!" Dad said, clearly not seeing the difference between "liking me" and "trampling me into the car seat."

I was too busy trying to protect my face with my arms to answer him. The dog was practically up on my shoulders, poking its nose into every gap, trying everything it could do to get past my hands so it could lick my face again.

"See, look how she's wagging her tail," Dad said.

Trumpet's ears were long and droopy and smooth. They looked as silky as my velvet dress.

"She *is* pretty" Mom said, as if she were looking for something nice to say.

"Of course she is. She's a beagle," Dad said. "Hey there, Trumpet. How's it going, girl?" He scratched behind her floppy ears.

"I like her!" Isaac announced.

"That's because she hasn't tried to lick your face off yet," I said. I glanced down at my dress. It was covered in little white and brown hairs. As the car started to move, before I could stop her, Trumpet curled up on my lap. She rolled onto her back like she was offering her belly to me.

"She wants you to rub her tummy," Isaac said. He reached over the bag and patted Trumpet's stomach.

"Are you sure? That's weird," I said.

"Isaac's right. Dogs like that," Dad said, peeking at us in the rearview mirror.

I gingerly touched Trumpet's pink and white stomach. It was much softer than I expected. I ran my fingers through the little whorls of short white fur. She wagged her tail and wriggled closer to me, resting her head on my free arm.

OK, I thought. *Maybe she is a little bit cute.*